I0682625

PREACHING
To
The
CRIEURS
T.D. GIDDENS
A Novel

Published in the United States by Dort Books
Publishing.

PREACHING TO THE CRIEURS

Sometimes, the ones preaching the loudest are the ones who need to hear preaching the most...

Six siblings, one wedding tangled in one unusual family. The Crieurs are preparing to celebrate the wedding of youngest sister, Naomi. Hope fades for a peaceful celebration when a bombshell threatens the nuptials.

Best described as the modern day film Soul Food, **Preaching To The Crieurs** *is packed with infidelity, romance and memorable characters.*

Preaching To The Crieurs *chronicles the lives of six Philadelphia, Pennsylvania siblings.*
Andre, the oldest of the Crieur siblings, is a ruthless and troubled soul.
Bethanny harbors resentment.
Pharah, the active Christian, leads the adult choir and does amazing work in her community.
Rachel, the reserved, middle sister, is in utter panic.
Cynthia is a stuck-up attorney who prides herself on hard work and aims to leave an impression for others to follow.
Naomi, the bride, and baby of the Crieur family, expects a baby of her own. She typically conceals her emotions to maintain the peace, but now she must choose between what she wants and what everyone else wants for her.

Will these powerful siblings cooperate long enough to prevent a nightmare? Or will their painful struggles and sordid pasts threaten to ruin what was supposed to be a blissful event?

Table of Contents

CHAPTER 1 Andre

WHACK! MY SISTER, CYNTHIA, FELL flat on the floor as soon as I plugged my fist into her face. It had been almost a year since we last spoke; and I used my last one dollar and forty cents of commissary to call Momma while being held in the County Jail on a drug charge when Cynthia answered instead.

"House of Beauty, this is Cutie; how may I help you?" she said with her *foul* attitude.

"What?"

Clearing her throat as if a bone were stuck in it, she said, "HEL-LO?"

"Put Momma on the phone, Cynthia!" I told her.

"Who, may I ask, is calling?"

"You don't know who this is?"

"Let us try this again, House of Beauty; this is Cutie, may I help you?" Cynthia said, "Or should I end the call, sir?"

"So now you call me, sir?" Before I could finish my sentence, I felt the sweat balls beading across my forehead. Heat filtered through the cracks of my skin.

"You've got to be kidding me! Are you for real, Cynthie?"

"It's CYNTH-I-A," she said, "WHO'S CALLING?"

I slammed the phone so hard, the mouthpiece cracked. That earned me a ticket in the hole that night. In a dark musty, stinky, rat hole behind metal bars of Houtzdale State Prison. My parents weren't sending me any money, and neither was Cynthia. If not for my wife, Monique, putting money in the commissary each month, I'd be in even more trouble. I made up my mind that night, no matter how much trouble I got myself into, Cynthia would pay one way or another.

And that's just what I did. I looked out the window of my parents' five-bedroom, Chestnut Hill, Philadelphia home. I saw her pull her driver's side mirrors in before prancing her boogie self into the house. Her mocha-brown skin was spray-painted with what she called makeup. I got nice and ready before I tiptoed to the corridor wedged between the wall and wooden door and waited for her to enter. She waltzed in with two Nordstrom Department Store shopping bags.

As she swung the door open, I balled my fist into position and lunged for her lips. The stinging from my knuckles didn't stop me from swinging a second jab to her head. She deserved it. With Cynthia out cold, I stared at her lifeless body.

She had a lot of guts when I called just a few months ago, but now she lay silent. Curled up on the floor with spots of blood on her white skirt, her black hair was pulled into a bun and her bags were sprawled across the floor. She was much taller than the last time I saw her. But within seconds, I was startled by loud screams coming from her fat lips.

"You're going to jail for this," she said.

She screamed louder. Loud enough to send me running out the front door. She should have known I wouldn't let her disrespect me like that. Bet she won't try to play me like an idiot again.

Chapter 2 Bethanny

I HAD BEEN SCREENING MY PHONE calls in hopes of avoiding Pharah's weekly reminder about *buying a dress* for Naomi's wedding. But now, I just trembled inside after I answered and gripped the edge of the cell phone as I pushed it closer to my ear.

"WHAT DID YOU SAY?" I replied to the anonymous woman on the other end of the phone, "HELLO? Are you still there?"

"How long have you been married, Bethanny?" the anonymous woman inquired. Her voice was unpleasant and scratchy as tin foil, which was just enough to unnerve me.

"How's that any of your business?" I replied, sitting on my sofa and watching my neighbor, Veronica, and my best friend, Sharon, who were seated across from me. Both were watching me closely.

"Did you know your husband was cheating?"

I hoped the anonymous woman wouldn't repeat her question if only to give me time to breathe. I needed a moment longer to process what she said. Sharon raised her eyebrows as if a mystery were about to unfold. I looked away.

"Are you there?" she said. "HELLO?"

"Where did you hear this information?"

"I didn't hear it," the anonymous woman said, "I saw him."

"You saw what?"

"I saw your husband with my OWN EYES," she replied. "Don't play stupid like you don't know what he's been up to. It's not like he comes home every day."

"He does come home every day," I told her, standing in the middle of the room and defending my words. Sunday, Monday, and Tuesday were his double time hours, when he left home by three p.m. and returned by nine the next morning.

"If he isn't working, he's at home with his family," I insisted.

The oven beeped from the kitchen, and my three-year-old son, Max, pounded his chest like Tarzan, "THE COOKIE'S READY, MOMMY."

Pushing the phone into my hip pocket, I replied, "I'm not too sure about that, honey. Maybe in two more minutes."

"You not sure about what, MOMMY?" Max said with disappointment in his eyes.

He looked at me, waiting for a killer reason as to why I would stand between him and his chocolate chip cookie. I wished he were with the two toddlers upstairs in my bedroom, dreaming about Mickey Mouse. Veronica stood up and mouthed to me, *Who is that?* I turned away from her and refocused on the voice at the other end of the phone.

"Hello?" the anonymous woman said. "He can't possibly take care of things at home with all the things he's doing for my cousin."

My chest cramped, and I felt dizzy.

"Don't tell me about what goes on in my own home!"

The voice in my head did a mean thing by reminding me of the reasons I should have taken Sharon up on her offer of a week-long girls' night out vacation without kids, husband, or drama. Guzzling down a glass of sangria on the warm beaches of Jamaica, under clear skies, beside translucent waters, were just some of the most valuable reasons to say yes to a departure from the family without any worry. Instead, my voice amplified how I was feeling.

"Alex takes care of his family," I said, "and real good too."

"He takes care of my cousin just as good, if not, better."

"I'm not going to sit here, listening to trash like you disparage what my husband and I have built together," I told her.

"Well, he's building something just as good with my cousin," the anonymous woman said. "Please don't think you're the only sweet, lovely, stay-at-home mother whose husband is committed, 'cause he's not."

Standing in front of my bay window, I watched the rain spattering on my car parked in the driveway. The smell of saturated dirt emanated from the screens of the open window. The quiet street of my suburban home had been disrupted. Letting my eyes roam up and down the street, I watched for unscrupulous visitors.

"You tell me what my husband does then," I challenged her. I was looking to sniff out her plot to sabotage my marriage, and added, "Since you think you know so much!"

"You'd be surprised at what I know."

"You don't know anything," I retorted.

"I know you have three kids," the woman said, "and you don't work, don't cook, and you shake your tail over at that club. Let's see… what's it called?"

"MOM-MY!" Max said as he suddenly stood in the middle of the room.

Cupping my hand over the mouthpiece of the phone, I said, "Sharon, get the cookies out of the oven," pointed Max toward the kitchen while Sharon followed after him.

Seated in silence, I listened to the anonymous woman breathing. *Shake your tail at the club? As in Roxy's strip club? The one I stripped at for five years and gave up to build a life with Alex? How'd she know? Was he embarrassed about it? Did he spread that around to people WE KNEW? Did he suddenly regret getting married to me? After five years?*

Scanned my brain, I searched for any memory of a time I suspected Alex might have lied.

"I know your husband don't like you," the anonymous woman said, "and he's only there for his kids, but that's about to change."

"Who are you?" I whispered, ashamed at her slithering, unwelcome voice intruding into my ear, and mind.

"Do you really want me to tell you anymore?" the woman asked.

I wanted to hang up, but part of me wanted to hear what she had to say. Sharon dumped the cookie tray on the table, and I swept the cookies into Kleenex tissues, using my shirtsleeve as a glove.

Max jumped up and down as if the cookies were his best friend. "MY COOKIES! MY COOKIES!" Veronica's eyes rested on mine.

They're all no good, Sharon mouthed to me about the man in my life whom I held dearest.

Sharon was willing to see me throw away the towel. I was not. I often thrilled myself over the knowledge that Alex was different from other men who cheat, lie, and leave their families. He stood by me, and never gave me any reason to distrust him. He provided everything he promised: a home and a family. Even though my own family didn't live up to their promises.

Sharon gestured for me to hang up, but I couldn't. Sharon's fiery red hair fell to her shoulders, and her glassy blue eyes showed fear.

"Give that baby some cookies," the anonymous woman said before her voice faded aways and the phone clicked.

"This chick hung up on me," I said. "Take me to Alex's job!" I screamed.

"Who was it?" Sharon said.

"Just take me to Alex's job," I begged.

Sharon grabbed her pocketbook and we headed out for the thirty-minute drive.

Chapter 3 Pharah

STARING IN THE BATHROOM mirror and examining my freshly brushed teeth, I decided they weren't as white as I would have liked. The two shots of espresso every Monday morning were beginning to show. My lower right tooth was brown, crooked, and awkward. It managed to make its own debut in every photo shot I'd ever taken. I hated it. So did everyone else, apparently, who came across my black face.

Even sales from the *Fortune Five Hundred* company I worked for slumped after our clients saw me face-to-face. "Pharah, you have such a nice," and then the dreaded pause. People were hesitant to compliment anything attached to my body. "You have such a nice personality!"

It was not much of a surprise to me since the odds of four girls in the same family being blessed with at least one favorable attribute would have been considered highly unlikely.

Pressing my right temple, I closed my eyes, "Ugh, God bless me with a wonderful companion."

Opening the bathroom cabinet, I grabbed the bottle of Tylenol Extra Strength, and popped one pill in before throwing the rest into my brown, crossover bag for backup. I'd already made six calls this morning to finalize my sister's wedding, and and managed to throw everything together as fast as she could say *I do*. I called the florist, booked a caterer, and had almost all the invited guest names embossed on the placement cards. After scheduling an appointment with a deejay in a matter of hours, the pulsing headache I was currently enduring could only become a setback to my already cramped schedule.

Ring! I hit the speaker button and placed the phone on top of the bathroom sink.

"Praise the Lord," I said.

"May I speak with Pharah Crieur, please?"

"This is Pharah,"

"Hi Pharah, it's John Baltic. I'm the account manager from Christian Mingle, the largest Christian dating website in the Delaware valley."

I laughed, and couldn't stop. That was my response: an overwhelming sense of relief to my four-year quest to find love. The constant chatter may finally have come to an end from my church choir, who thought it was a great idea to sign me up for a dating website. It may not have been such a bad idea after all. I dropped my bag on the floor and smiled at my reflection in the mirror.

"Oh, hello John, and thank you for calling me back."

"Well, I'm excited, Pharah, that you've chosen our website to start your dating search. Just let me know how I can be of help?" he said.

Where do I begin? FIND ME A DATE. The men I'm interested in aren't interested in me. I haven't been kissed in ten years, and the only guy I went very far with ran off. It doesn't help that my black skin, crooked teeth, and thick hair stand out more than *my personality.* I stepped into my bedroom and dropped myself onto the queen-sized bed. "Let's see… The site doesn't give me the option to select what I want in a potential date," I told him, sitting up on my bed, and kicking my shoe off.

"Have you created a profile page?"

"Yes. I have," I said, "at least, part of it."

I purposely skipped out on Bingo the very night it was created, but after nine hours of toying with it, everything on the monitor became a blur.

"That's one step," he said.

"There are certain things I really would like to eliminate right off."

I made my introduction as simple as possible. Momma said the reason I'm not dating was because I'm too pushy, too friendly, and too friendly toward the wrong people. She suggested that I use the same sales tactics that I used at work to land a date.

"There are other options," he said.

Other options… like how? Can I get dark chocolate, muscular, God-fearing person delivered by mail order?

I shook the steamy figure right out of my head. "The other issue is: I'm not particularly excited about the requirement that I list my age."

Age was as private as my Social Security number. It took twenty-eight years to attain it, and revealing it to the world wasn't appropriate.

13

"We don't always require individuals to answer that question. If you're more comfortable in exaggerating your age, then that's fine," he said.

My mind was in a buzz.

"Exaggerating my age?" I said. The Tylenol hadn't kicked in yet. I wished it would, not only to relieve the pain, but now, the aggravation.

"That doesn't sound encouraging," I said, "but I'm willing to make it work."

One date could only be squeezed in between choir rehearsal on Thursday, community action on Friday, and volunteering at the nursing homes on Tuesday afternoons. I nearly gloated at the idea of being in love. Having hugs, snuggles, and cuddles.

"Pharah, it sounds like you are ready to make the commitment to start a whole new chapter in your life. If I'm reading your email correctly, you are interested in a college graduate, who cooks, and no children; am I correct?"

Scratching my temple, I replied, "Yes, but you left out no smoking, no cursing, and no lying. He must be baptized, attend church regularly, and pays his tithes," I insisted.

He gasped, but I continued. "I wanted to add some additional criteria, but the site doesn't allow that." I imagined Momma pulling my ears for being pushy again.

"You are also having trouble uploading your pictures, is that correct?" he said, "and posting photos of you smiling?"

OH NO! Did I have any photos without the monstrous teeth? I switched the call to speaker in order to scour through my phone for a picture.

"Well, I have tons," I said.

"Light backgrounds?"

The brown tooth danced around in my head. "I don't have many pictures of me smiling, but I do have bright backgrounds."

"Have you received any feedback from the ones you've already uploaded?"

"No." And there it was. The reality of nine hours dedicated to finding a date; yet still, no hit.

"Try changing your cover photo is my suggestion. The page takes a few days to update; so be patient and keep checking back in." He added, "You should be on your way to finding love in no time,

14

Pharah." He chuckled, but my sense of humor had already disappeared. "Good luck with everything, Pharah."

Patting my forehead dry, I poked my fingers into the kinky locks and teased them into place. My phone buzzed again from the edge of the bed. Rachel's name popped across the phone screen. Rachel and Bethanny were two of the worst appointment keepers ever. They gave new meaning to the warning, *one should never make plans with family or for family.*

If it wasn't their constant whining about what "they had to do" or how I was "inconveniencing their lives," or "they didn't have any money," or "were too busy," it was some other nonsense. After waiting two days, she finally called me back. I let out a sigh.

"I fell asleep," Rachel said after I answered.

"Where have you been?"

"I'm home with Ashley. She wasn't feeling well," she said. And she was that quick to blame her kid for her own bad behavior.

"Be ready for the fittings at eleven on Wednesday," I said.

"Have you seen her?" Rachel asked.

Silence descended, and I knew the dreaded question would slip in somehow, but not this soon. Rolling my eyes, I dropped my head backwards and landed on the bed.

"Seen who?" I asked.

"Elsie?"

"No!" I replied abruptly. "Be ready at eleven a.m. Talk to you later."

ELSIE. Ten years later, and her name still creeped me out. I always knew this day would come. *ELSIE.* I managed to avoid her for a total of ten-and-a-half years. *Successfully.* I sent all of her calls to voicemail, returned her letters unopened, and refused to let her name fall from my lips. But she was here. At my mother's house, eating my parents' food, sleeping in my old bedroom with *her kids* and the *husband.* The kids who should have been *my* kids, with the *husband* who promised to be mine. *She stole him.*

My cat, Cattle, rubbed her black fur against my leg. "Give Mommy a kiss," I whispered. "There's someone out there for me, right, Cattle?" I said, "There has to be."

Chapter 4 Rachel

TAKING A SEAT IN THE mahogany-colored sofa closest to the door, I went for my nails, and bit them anxiously. I promised myself I'd complete the forty-five-minute session without walking out.

"How have you been, Rachel?" Dr. Choi asked.

He smiled from behind his desk. Doctor Choi was an average-sized Asian man, no taller than five-foot-two. His ebony-black hair was parted in the middle. Wearing a white lab coat, his eyeglasses were pushed far enough down on his nose to make his eyes look foggy from where I sat. He held his head close to the desk, suggesting to me he was as bored with me as I was with him. I tapped my foot on the red carpet.

"I'm feeling good."

The musty smell of Dr. Choi's cologne permeated the room. His framed licenses hung on the wall above his head. I focused my attention on them whenever I could.

"Are you up to talking today?" he asked gleefully, "It's been two weeks. Are you warming up yet? You still have to discuss why you shut down. That's the only way you will overcome this," he said.

I bit deeper into my nail. "I know," I whispered.

He paused between sentences and said, "Um-hum" before beginning the next, "Have you read any of the literature I suggested?"

"Yeah," I said, "I've skimmed through some of it."

"Um-hum' did your skimming provide any relief or assistance?"

"Just a little," I lied.

"I see," he said. "Have you been meditating at all, Rachel? It helps alleviate stress."

"Well, I haven't tried yet," I said, "but I do plan to."

"The breathing exercise?"

"Yeah," I said, "I tried that too." I didn't dare admit falling asleep in the middle of practicing.

"Um-hum. Good," he said, "I have a bit more literature I'd like you to look over. It might play an intricate part of your recovery."

Recovery?

I crossed my leg over the other, and stared at Dr. Choi until he said, "Are you okay?"

"Yes," I replied, "I'm fine."

"Well, I know in our meeting last week, you said this all may have started because your father announced your presence at his church?"

I closed my eyes, trying to erase the memory of my first experience with anxiety. I pressed my eyes tightly shut. I thought Pastor's seven-year absence wasn't supposed to affect me. It never had before. Even when we only lived two miles from one another, and at times, when I stood in the same room of his home, but he'd never look at me. I got over it though; at least, I thought I did.

"Do you want to begin where we left off?" Dr. Choi asked. "We'll have to cover some things in order to get to the bottom of what's really bothering you."

Dr. Choi placed his pen on the table, as if waiting for my next move. "Our minds are like machines," he said, "if there's too much buildup, the machine will crash from the over flow."

"So am I overflowing?" I said. The pressures in my life seemed to have overflowed twenty times during the past few weeks.

"Are you, Rachel?"

"I don't know. I guess," I answered.

Forcing myself back to the day, three weeks ago, when I sat in church services where Daddy, the pastor, stood on the podium and addressed over two hundred congregates. It was my first time there in eight years, which was when he cut me out of his life. My original plan was to quietly creep into the back pews, remaining farthest away from everything and everyone, but still be present to support Momma when she announced Naomi's wedding to the church.

I came there unbeknown, and undisturbed by Pastor's loyal audience, his followers, whom he decided long ago came before all else.

And then my father, the pastor, said, "Welcome back, Rachel. We missed you."

Everyone stood up and stared at me. The cheers, clapping, and laughter from the room of big hats and suits drove me into a sheer panic. I shook, and the air inside my lungs sucked right out. I held Ashley tightly on my lap, gripping her body close to mine.

Gasping for air, I struggled to breathe. Darkness fell, and I woke up a few hours later at Torresdale Hospital with Momma's hands held over me in prayer.

"Um-hum," Dr. Choi said. "Whom do you live with?"

"My daughter. Just my daughter, Ashley, and me."

"How old is Ashley?" Dr. Choi inquired as he lowered his chin and focused his attention more obviously on me.

"She's five years old."

"Um-hum. Do you have thoughts of harming yourself or others?"

Define harm? Be specific, mister. Can I harm myself if I don't feel harmed? "Not really. I mean, no." I said.

Dr. Choi quickly jotted down his notes on a long, white, legal pad as if he were having trouble following every word I said.

"I see," he said. "Have you been under a lot of stress lately?

"Well, of course, I am the single mother of a five-year-old child."

"Um-hum. Are you in a relationship? Is there a significant person in your life?"

"Yes, I mean, no. But I have a friend."

"What kind?" he looked closer at me.

"A friend-friend" I reiterated without going X-rated. My good friend, Carson Ellis, visited me often for our regular weekly encounters. If it weren't for Ashley, we'd have met even more often.

"How's the relationship?"

"I don't consider it a relationship; he's just someone I see here and there. We are working on one. But it's pretty tough,"

"Um-hum," he said. "Is he abusive?"

"No."

"Is he the father of your child?"

I shook away the nerves that crept beneath my skin. Jittery. Irritated. The feelings of angst brewed within.

"No," I said, "her father is not really in the picture."

"Um-hum. Is he in contact with you or the child?"

I folded my hands together. "He's making things a little difficult, I guess," I said.

"What is he doing to make things difficult?"

"He just thinks he should run things even though he hasn't really been there for Ashley."

"Um-hum."

"He's tough to deal with at times," I cracked my knuckles.

"Have you reached a resolution yet?"

I shrugged, positioning my hands over my face to calm the whispers in my head that screamed, *Run, Rachel! Just run!*

"Yes," I said, "I mean, no, we are still working out the details. He wants to work it out."

"It's okay, Rachel," he said. "Take a deep breath." I crossed, then uncrossed my legs. Leisurely rocking, I hugged my knees.

"Are you okay?" Dr. Choi asked.

I nodded to reassure him. "Yes. Of course," I said.

"Um-hum. Do you want to continue?"

"Yes, I'm fine."

"Okay, are you employed?"

"Yes, I work at a teen shelter," I said, "a shelter for girls. It pays my bills. Sometimes, it's hard to keep my head above water, you know, with Ashley and all." I nervously rubbed my hands together before I continued. "Single motherhood, of course, is stressful. I love my daughter; she's so cute; but it's hard raising a child by yourself. No one is there to support you, not even the one who helped conceive the child; no one ever stays."

Dr. Choi stopped writing and glanced at me, "You can go on, Rachel?"

"I know I had her at a young age, and probably shouldn't have been having sex. I know she's my responsibility, and I've disappointed a lot of people. It's no one else's problem but mine," I finished. Crossing my legs again, I closed my eyes. "No one ever says what a good job I'm doing," I continued. "No one offers to baby sit, or pats me on my back, and sometimes, it's rough," I let out a sigh.

"Um-hum. I see," he said. "Whom are you referring to when you say *no one?*"

"I'm done." I shook my head and bit into what was left of my thumb nail.

"Do you want to stop now? We have another ten minutes to go. We can change the subject if you like."

Wiping the tear from my eye, I replied, "No, you can go ahead, Doctor Choi."

Chapter 5 Cynthia

THE LINES IN THE COURTHOUSE extended out the door. The chirping sound that came from my briefcase as it rolled down the metal detector annoyed me. The smell of stale cigarettes swirled around the uniformed guard whose handheld detector scrolled over my back. I waited two days before I decided to pick up the court order, which would probably make a lot of people besides my lousy brother angry.

"Can I help you, ma'am?" the clerk behind the glass counter asked politely.

"Yes," I replied. "I'm Cynthia Crieur, *Attorney* Cynthia Crieur. I'm here to pick up a court order."

"What's the party's name?"

"Cynthia Crieur versus Andre Crieur," I replied.

Pulled off my dark sunglasses, I gave the clerk a good look at my blackened eye, if only to shame my brother, Andre, who thought it was okay to hit me with his bare hand. *Hitting me!* A woman of my caliber! And without just cause.

"Okay, Miss Crieur," she said, "this is a protection from abuse complaint, correct?"

"Absolutely, "

"Give me a sec."

She stood up and held the bottom of her bulging gut in as she tiptoed to the back of the office. Her hair was braided down her back in cornrows. She hummed to a tune from the O'Jay's that blared from the radio stationed on her desk.

Looked around the room, I soon found a green-eyed jiggler whose attention appeared to be fixed in my direction. The olive-colored man was doing some weird moves with his head. He nodded, as if trying to get my attention. I rolled my eyes. "Get a life," I muttered.

The woman returned and took her seat, handing me a sealed envelope file. She said, "You'll have to serve him with his court appearance."

I opened my mouth to protest, but snapped it shut before saying, *Me? Just so he can attack me again?*

"A family member or police escort will also suffice," the desk clerk added.

The sooner I got over to Momma's, the sooner I could get this mess over with, although Momma refused to help, and none of my siblings would have. They would have preferred to give me a speech on why I should just scrap the whole restraining order altogether since it could result in him going back to jail.

"You'll need to pay the twenty-five dollar fee today," she said.

I pressed my lips together tightly, figuring my protest wasn't with her as I whipped out my credit card and handed it to the woman. "Now he's costing me money," I grumbled. The woman looked at me with a *what'd you say?* look. "Never mind," I said, flagging her off.

So much for living a simple life. *Working hard. Doing good deeds...* When the time arrives, in return, good things should happen. Not like my siblings who are always waiting for someone else's help. Pharah can't find a man because she thinks she's Miss Holier-Than-Thou and is so full of herself. Bethanny's married, but so wrapped up on that short husband, she can't find her way in life. She should take a chapter out of my book. That's the reason I've taken a *timeout* from my ex-boyfriend, Dr. Terrance Wolsom, an emergency room doctor at Jefferson Hospital. He's too clingy, too touchy, and over the top with everything except the simple things I want. He failed my focus test. *Focus on me when I need you.* That's truly where he went wrong.

Rachel's always broke because she won't go back to school in order to get a real job, one with benefits for Ashley and her. Andre, well, he'll never amount to anything as long as he keeps stuffing white powder up his nose, and that'll never change. Naomi had a small chance of making it, but let some part-time mechanic screw her future away. As if getting married would change anything about his coins.

"Stop being so critical!" Momma yelled at me when I began telling her the truth about her offspring. She says, the more I badmouth, the less good things happen for me. That's a lie. I'm happily single. Just check with Dr. Terrance, my former love bug whose blue eyes and blonde hair weren't enough to prevent me from commanding an early dismissal. He patiently awaits my telephone call, which won't ever come until he adheres to focusing. That's another reason I'm shielding myself from selfish idiots. I'm employed and have enough of my own coin that I never feel the need to share it.

But I reminded Momma of her favorite adage she said to me when I was a kid: "Tell the truth to shame the devil." The truth taught me to grow a thick skin, want more, and do better. That's just the reason why I'm not going to listen to her view on why her kids aren't living the lives they should. I signed my credit card receipt and returned it to the woman behind the desk. "Good riddance," I said.

Walking out of the building into the noisy street of Downtown Center City Philadelphia's Tuesday morning roar, I heard the loud voices echoing down the street, and the car horns beeping. Music blared from a maroon Honda Accord parked in the fire lane outside the courthouse. I walked by the car where a slender, curly-haired young man sat.

He stared back at me from the corner of his eye, and I turned my head to signal, *I'm not interested.* He shot up from the driver's seat, resting his right arm on the steering wheel where I saw a tattoo of a broken cross. He moved quickly, but I was still unsure of his intent.

His beard was trimmed and brushed neatly. His hazel brown eyes stayed squarely riveted on mine. Poking his head out the window, he asked, "Oh, so you just intend to run right by me?"

I ignored the flagrantly annoying soul who presumably was without any direction. "Yo, Cynthia!" he said, "What's up? That's how you do me?"

I turned to get a better look at the strange person, still acting quite aloof. He held both his arms out like I was causing him great pain. His voice was familiar, but his *face*? Not so much. Not much in the way of eye candy either, but I wanted to know who was throwing my name around *so loudly in* public.

"You don't remember me?" he asked as he stepped out of the car like he was releasing the weight of the world from his lap.

"Um, no," I said. "Who are you?"

I removed my dark sunglasses, but quickly placed them back on, moving closer toward him for a better view. "Oh, wow! What's up, James?" I said.

The voice was as familiar to me as George Washington High School, my alma mater. James Ingrid was one of four hundred in our graduating class, but one of the few who took his dentistry very seriously. His teeth were straight as a ruler. His lips? Smooth, and plump. And his bad, boyish, "I'm so cool" hood-style of speaking was, unbelievably, refreshingly welcoming.

"Didn't know that was you."

He wrapped his long arms around my back. His warm body smelled of Calvin Klein's Mist cologne, my favorite, and I would've welcomed the cool scent much more if it were minus the smell of marijuana.

CHAPTER 6 NAOMI

"NAOMI!" MOMMA YELLED FOR ME to come downstairs. I'd only been there for twenty minutes and she was already at it.

"I'm coming," I replied.

Stretching my arm across the pillow top mattress and white down comforter, I saw my cream-colored wedding gown hanging on the back of the door. I stared at the pink walls that once held posters of Rihanna and Mylie Cyrus, a mute testimony of my *puberty*. I felt like capturing a minute more of what I'd missed in the past three months. Ever since Pastor decided he didn't want an unmarried, single woman's big, pregnant belly waddling around his house while he stood behind a podium every Sunday and preached against it. I obliged, and invited myself back for a visit only after Momma announced Norman had asked me to marry him, even though he *technically* hadn't.

If your mom and dad want us to get married, then let's do it, Norman said two months earlier. That was after I cried for two weeks once I realized my period, which arrived like clockwork on the twenty-ninth day of the month, every month, failed to deliver. That caused a divide I wasn't prepared for, and that was the essence of our engagement.

Momma set the wedding date while Pastor announced the wedding ceremony guidelines:

Reception in the basement of Calvary Baptist Church.

*No booze. No music. Church melodies only (*Momma gave me the right to select only one*), and church member invitees only.*

Boring.

Boring wasn't part of the guidelines, but my parents should have included it as a reminder to my guests and me. It's not the wedding I planned, but neither was my current living arrangement.

Sleeping in Cynthia's twin bed in her guest bedroom didn't do much for me right now, but as she said, "Beggars can't be picky."

I couldn't live with Norman yet, since Pastor was against that too. Momma wanted me to move back home. She said it will help bring my blood pressure down to normal since my doctor says I'm

24

not relaxed enough. Her feelings don't matter, however, when Pastor sets down the house rules. The Crieur family house rules were *permanently* applicable, even for a twenty-one-year-old who still dreamt about living happily ever after.

Norman didn't share my happily-ever-after dreams. His tan skin, bowed legs, (as wide as a grasshopper's), and short stature seemed to contradict physics. Even though I didn't find him attractive, his sense of humor helped me do what I knew how to do best: to go with it. So I did. I've done that all of my life. And at times, Norman's been against me more often than I care to admit.

"I'm coming, Mother!" I said.

Jessa's fist, or what I assumed was her fist, stuck out of Norman's tee shirt. It was now my makeshift maternity dress. Her distinctive body part poked out of my stomach like an alien, trying to hatch from its shell. I rubbed the center of my belly and hoped to soothe her morning activities. With only one month left, I was more anxious than ever to finally meet her.

"NAOMI" Momma's voice echoed louder than the last call.

Jumped out of the bed, I used my hands as a back brace to keep my posture in an upright position. A knock at the door followed. "Come in," I said.

"Your mother's calling you, Naomi," Elsie told me as she opened the door.

Elsie was a girl who once needed a safe place to go. Momma took her in after Rachel brought her home. She was previously living in one of those teen shelters without any family or support. My parents loved how she trooped to church every Sunday to hear the word despite her problems. However, the word she stole something of Pharah. But no one talked about that. She'd been married now for about two years, and came back here to visit; but I believed she just came here to be nosy like the rest of Momma's friends.

Elsie's pink rollers jutted out of her coffee-black hair. Her black satin cap extended down the back of her hair. The red bathrobe she insisted on wearing could easily have been mistaken for Elmo's. She patted her head.

I rubbed my eyes and slipped on my pink bedroom slippers as I hurried to the door. "I'm coming down," I said.

"How are you feeling?" Elsie asked. I plopped myself back on the bed, temporarily saved by her questions.

"I'm feeling good," I said.

"I'm taking the girls to the mall. They need pantyhose and barrettes; would you like to come?" she inquired.

Elsie asked me to go the mall twice since I've been here. I gave her the same answer each time. Along with my doomed wedding, my mother's constant nagging, and her incessant questions, I felt like I was part of a tag team whose mission was *how to get Naomi aggravated.*

"Um no," I said, "I don't think I need anything."

I wish they'd all just shut up, and let me be. Jessa kicked again. Her magic power to deform my one-hundred-and-sixty-eight-pound body was quite enough for one person. Less than two weeks still to go, and then this whole wedding thing would be over, thank God.

"How long are you staying?"

"Maybe for two more weeks," Elsie replied. "We'll leave right after the wedding."

What wedding? Who invited you? My slanted eyes refused to blink.

"Your mother invited me," she added as if reading my mind.

Momma keeps trimming and growing my wedding list. I would have settled for just me at the altar. Marrying my own voice. *"Naomi, will you take your own VOICE as your lawfully wedded husband?"* Pastor will ask. *And I'll say, "Yes, I do."*

"Is the baby kicking yet?" Elsie asked.

I lifted Norman's white shirt and exposed Jessa's alien body part, poking from my stomach. "Yeah, she kicks."

"Oh? It's a girl?"

"Yes, Jessa."

"It's a beautiful name. Her nickname should be Jess," Elsie said.

I smiled, wondering if I asked for her suggestion, or was she offering it because she knew, like everyone else who kept planning my life, that I'd just listen?

"Are you excited about your wedding?"

"Where're your daughters?" I replied.

There. The *none of your business, skip your questions* was unrelated to her stare. Questions my mother wouldn't seem to stop asking, and which I ignored and refused to talk about. Where could I find an empty space to scream?

"*NAOMI*," my mother called for me.

"Let me go down there and see what she wants."

"Will your sister be here today?"

"Yes. I guess," I shrugged. "I guess she will."

I took my time going down the stairway. Gripping the handrails to keep my wobbling legs steady, I hurried into the kitchen. So much for staying relaxed.

CHAPTER 7 Rachel

I DABBED MY CHEEKS WITH the back of my hand. Doctor Choi was really giving me a run for my money. So much for my plan to keep quiet for most of my visit. But my tears wouldn't stop.

There was a chance Pastor would cut me off for good if I decided to keep Ashley, but at the time, I was ready to take that risk. She possesses everything I lack; meaning, she's bubbly, sweet, and forgiving.

"Your male friend, does he help you with Ashley?" Dr. Choi inquired.

I twitched my nose a bit after thinking of Carson helping out in one way or another with Ashley. He hasn't ever acknowledged it, but I sense he has an allergy to little people. That was one of the reasons our three-days-per-week trysts slimmed down to one. And always owing to my urgent needs, rather than his.

"He is not around my daughter," I said. Sitting up straighter, to defend my position, I added, "I mean, I let her around him, but not without me."

"Um-hum."

"You know what I mean," I said, "he's not her father,"

"Do you trust him?"

"Trust? Like what?" I said, slumping into the chair.

"Are you trusting of him?" Dr. Choi repeated.

"We've been seeing each other for a couple of weeks, so it's nothing serious like that. He hasn't mentioned being serious."

"Are you two sexually active?"

"Yeah," I replied.

Wishing I hadn't answered as fast as I did, I thought, maybe he'll figure out that I've never gone without a sexual partner for longer than two months. As Doctor Choi reviewed his questions, I couldn't help sneaking into my past. Struck by the trees waving from outside Dr. Choi's office window, the branches seemed to be praising the massive earth nourishing it. The sun shone brightly one early morning, on my way to school, when I stopped for him.

"You need a ride?" the man asked after rolling the window down of his silver Mazda. Nice car, nice hair, nice smile. I nodded. "Get in," he said. So I did.

"Shorty, you got pretty eyes," he told me after I sat down in the front passenger seat beside him, warmed by the heated leather seat beneath me.

"Where are you headed?" he asked.

"Lincoln High School,"

"They won't miss you today, will they," he asked.

His smile was wide as the moon, and his caramel skin brightened the car's interior. The smell of spice wafted from his direction, reminding me of Pastor's Old Spice, but with a touch of apple scent. I was glad Pharah decided to stay home that morning. That left me alone with a handsome jewel.

"Kareem," he said as he extended his hand and I took it. "You?"

"Rachel."

"Oh, that's a pretty name. I could spot those bold legs anywhere," he said, "You work out, don't you?"

"No."

Popping his eyes from the road to me every few seconds, I smiled from the inside out, wishing I had more to say. Deejays Roger and Sandborne's voices cheered through the car speakers. I felt warmed by the idea of driving in his car. Twisting my size six waist into the chair, I took another peek at him to make sure I wasn't dreaming again.

"So you want to hang out with me?" he asked.

"It doesn't matter," I said. His warm smile made me feel safe.

"Cool."

"Just make sure you bring me back to school before the last bell rings," I said.

"Don't worry," he said, "I got you, Shorty."

I was his *Shorty*. I smiled at the sound of it. He talked more about himself, and I sat silent and listened.

He rolled the car windows down to let the cool fall breeze fill the interior. We pulled in front of a store with awnings that projected from its roof. The peeling letters on the side of the building read, "Reem Ribs." There were a few chairs outside. It sat among row homes on the crowded street, and people were everywhere. A crowd waited to board a public transportation bus.

Kareem caught my eye. His peculiar, once bright, eyes darkened. For a second, I paused in regret over not going to school. Kareem walked around to my side of the car and opened the door. I exited. My once white canvases were now dirty, so I smacked them with my left hand and stood by bumper.

"Come on," he said, "we hanging out."

He led me into the storefront vestibule where we stood behind a second door to what looked like an apartment. Kareem instructed me to wait while he ran up the stairs, so I did.

He came down a few minutes later, wearing a dingy cloth that he wrapped around his sweaty neck. He led me up the stairs into a small, but tidy studio. The space was wide. The white walls in the living area held ample displays of art, and the mustard-brown cabinets in the kitchen and an open bathroom door were all visible from the studio entry where I stood.

As he led me in, he gestured for me to sit on the black leather sofa, so I did. We made small talk: his car, his kids, and his money, while I did my best to wrap my mind around his handsome smile. Reflecting on how it could be if we shared a child together, I decided the baby's wavy hair would most certainly have been guaranteed his daddy's good looks.

He removed his red shirt, leaving only his white tank top. His broad shoulder muscles exploded from his shirt. I kicked my shoes off while he went from the bedroom into the kitchen. All the while, he kept asking about my school. I'd never actually gone into a boy's house without my parents, but I didn't feel out of place. Kareem sat near me and flicked through the television channels.

After a few minutes into The Three Stooges, he said, "You look good as heck, girl. I smiled and pulled my skirt over my knees. "I haven't met a chick like you in over a minute."

I giggled underneath my blushing. "Oh, whatever; you probably say that a lot," I said.

Kareem leaned into the sofa. "Naw, for real, girl. You got a sexy walk," he said, "and I wanted you from the moment I saw you. What's that?" he asked, leaning close enough that I could smell his onion breath.

He was pointing to my wrist. I placed my hand over the quarter-sized scar on the back of my hand. It was permanently there from horsing around over a lit stove. Placing his hands over mine, he tightened his grip.

"YES SIR!" Kareem suddenly said. He shouted loud enough to make me jump away from where we sat. "Get in HERE!" he said. His eyes wandered around the room. Unsure of what he was doing, since he knelt only a few inches away, I pulled my wrist to free myself, but he gripped tighter. He looked over his shoulder. So did I.

"Hey," I said, "that hurts!"

My heart raced faster than I could think. Kareem looked around anxiously, then whispered, "It'll go real smooth if you just relax, Shorty."

Shooting up from the sofa, I felt helpless when he pushed me back down on it.

"Hey! Let go, Kareem, that really hurts," I protested.

I squirmed and fought to twist away, but his grip was tenacious. I bit into his hands, and he punched my lips.

"Stop!" I shrieked. The stinging in my mouth couldn't distract me from the blood dripping down my shirt. I continued to kick and scream, but Kareem used his thigh to pin me back down onto the sofa.

"Abu! Man, come on!" he said.

"Party time" A naked man, presumably Abu, appeared behind Kareem with his cell phone in hand. I let out a scream. Kareem placed the palm of his hand over my mouth. Using my forehead as a weapon, I threw my head at his chest. He punched me again. I screamed louder.

The naked, greasy, coffee bean-black Abu stood over me. His penis was exposed. Kareem grabbed my wrist over my head, and pinned me tightly to the sofa. But I screamed.

"Stop it!" I yelled. "What are you doing?" *Will they find me? They'll never forgive me! I have to get home!* "Oh my God, please stop!" I cried.

The two continued tossing me around. My screams weren't loud enough. I used my knees to push my lower body. Kareem held my hands over my head.

His left hand ripping my shirt off, Kareem warned me. "Quiet down girl!"

31

The naked Abu came face-to-face with me and pulled me by my shoulder. "Please, stop it," I pleaded. "Why are you doing this?"

Kareem pushed his hand farther into my mouth. "If you don't shut up, I'm going to kill you," he said.

His hand tasted of salt as his sweaty palms lay over my mouth. I tearfully kicked and wiggled my body as the naked Abu kissed my neck. I churned from side-to-side, tiring myself helplessly with every push. As they mercilessly ripped each garment from my body, I could feel the cold draft of air on my naked skin. I let go and went limp as the two took turns having sex with me.

I prayed to live, then I prayed for forgiveness, and finally prayed for the pain to end. Tears rolled down my face, I held my breath each time Kareem pushed himself deeper inside me. His eyes were empty and dark. The brightness in his eyes was gone, leaving only a black emptiness. He held my arms tightly against him and shook until he was done.

"You are a pretty girl," he said. "Maybe you can give us a treat, Rach?" he said, pointing to his penis.

"Abu, man, what do you think?"

Abu dragged his erect penis over my lips like windshield wipers wiping away the rain. I lay stiffly on the sofa and closed my eyes. I only opened them after Kareem demanded that I dress. The two dropped me off on the empty school grounds.

"When can we do this again?" Abu asked sarcastically. He stepped out of the backseat of the car. I walked home and waited until everyone went to bed before I showered, crying softly as the water hit my body.

"Rachel?" Dr. Choi said. Batting my eyelashes a few times, I had to remember where Dr. Choi and I left off. "I think that's all for today," he said. He looked at the clock that ticked over my head. "I think you need to make some time for yourself, young lady," he added. "Some quiet time just for you."

"Okay, can I call you to reschedule?" I asked. "I'm meeting with my family this weekend and the next few weeks will be very busy. My sister's wedding. I don't know if I will be able to squeeze in counseling."

"That sounds like an exciting time ahead for you" he said. "You'll get to relax. How about we schedule for next Tuesday, and if you can't keep the appointment, just call my office to cancel?"

"Okay," I said, "I guess that works."

"I don't think you should let more than a week go by without seeing me, Rachel" he added. "Are your anxieties any better?"

Better? Than what? I thought. *Better since yesterday?*

"Yes," I replied.

"Um-hum," he said, "good,"

"I'll call you first thing if I can't make it," I promised as I hurried out of the office.

CHAPTER 8 Bethanny

THE RAIN STOPPED and muggy air replaced it. During the late summer, the air becomes thick and misty. The music in the Dodge minivan was stationed on hardcore gangster rap, but that didn't keep me from crying. I wiped sweat from my forehead and Sharon thumped her fist on the steering wheel as she drove. We pulled into the parking lot of the Esquire building, and I walked into the grand lobby first. The twenty-foot ceilings couldn't compare to the tall glass of nonsense the anonymous woman kept trying to make me swallow.

After signing the visitor log that was located at the main entrance, I approached the desk to ask the officer to page Alex. He often greeted me right there, on his usual second shift, whenever I delivered his hot dinners. Then we'd stand under the building fountain and share our dreams for our family.

"Buy a bigger house," he often said, "and we'll have more kids, and hire a nanny" to help me.

"Can you page my husband, please?" I asked the officer.

Al, the desk officer, said, "Oh, Alex is off today, ma'am." I looked in Al's eyes for any sign of deception as my legs suddenly turned to jelly.

"He's not here, dear."

"Well, he did come to work today, didn't he?" I persisted.

"No, sweetheart. Alexus is off until Tuesday," he said as he dropped the clipboard on the desk.

I'd spoken to Alex only two hours earlier, just before he left for his ten p.m. shift. He was wearing his uniform.

"This may be off the cuff, sir, but when was the last time he showed up to work?" Sharon inquired.

"Alexus has been on vacation for, let's see, about two weeks now. Let me make sure," he pulled his clipboard closer to his hairy face. His salt and pepper hair was slicked back and his dry-cleaned shirt held a wad of pens in the pocket. His belly stuck out prominently. "Yes," he said, "it says here he's been out for couple of weeks. Said he was taking the family to Jamaica."

My eyes felt heavy as they filled with tears. I quickly wiped them away, however.

"What family?" I asked. "Are you sure?"

"Well, of course, dear," he replied. "One of the other guards was heading to Jamaica too, so I know for sure that's where he said he went."

"They're all supposed to be going there together?" I asked incredulously.

"Well, that I don't know, I just know there were a few folks going to the Caribbean several weeks ago." He propped his back against the chair and put his hands behind his head. "Nice place to vacation, though."

"Did he say who his family was?" Sharon said.

Al's puzzled expression preceded his next question. "What's your name dear?" he asked.

"I'm Bethanny Everett," I said. "I'm his wife."

"Well, I suppose he was referring to you as his family?"

"No," I said, "I don't know where he is." Snatching my phone from my pocket, I dialed Alex, and his voicemail immediately picked up.

"Alex, honey, this is an emergency," I said, "I need you to call me as soon as possible. *It's an emergency!"* I hung up and addressed the desk officer again, "Thanks for your help, sir."

"I'm sorry, dear. Looks like Alexus got himself into a bind. Wish I could tell you anything else about him, but he and I don't discuss his family very much."

Marching back to the car, my phone rang, and I answered.

"Your husband is with my cousin," the anonymous woman said.

"What the hell are you talking about?" I replied angrily. "Who are you?"

"Alex is at the Silver Lounge Motel on Patterson Avenue in Room twenty-two with my cousin. They just checked in and you can take a guess at what they're doing!" The woman let out a sinister laugh.

"No, they're not!" I retorted. "I know about chicks like you! You're just trying to be me, and live like me, because you wish you were me." The woman laughed loudly. But I wouldn't let up.

"You're another jealous, crazy whore, that's all!" I said. "Y'all are vultures and would do anything to get a man, even if he's married."

"Is that her?" Sharon ripped the phone from my hand "Now talk to this!" she exclaimed, ending the torture before she returned the phone to me.

"There's no way!" I said, "no way, I'm telling you, there's just no way he could do this!" I was determined to fight a battle I didn't ask for. I redialed Alex.

"What did she say?" Sharon asked.

"Alex, you need to call me back; this is an emergency, and I don't know where the hell you are. I just came from your job and they said you're not there!" I fumed. "What the hell is going on, Alex? You need to call me back right now!"

Standing eye-to-eye with Sharon, I begged, "It's not true, right? Do you really think he would do that to me? He couldn't, right?"

"I don't know, Bethanny, but we sure will find out. Give me your phone." Sharon skimmed the phone for the last call received and dialed the anonymous woman's number.

"She's not answering. What kind of game is she playing?" Sharon asked. I sat on the hood of my car, rubbing my hands together before my body went as numb as my heart.

"She said Alex is laying up at the Silver Lounge."

"What?" Sharon said, "What lounge?"

"She says her cousin is with him."

"Which lounge?" she repeated. I was too embarrassed to say it, since it was *our* anniversary, birthday and getaway lounge.

"There's only one."

"Not *thee* one?"

Slamming my hand on the hood of my car, "Yes," I said, "that one, Sharon. There's no way he could do this to me!"

"Well, what do you want to do in retaliation?"

Kill her. Kill them. Then me, but who'd take my three angels? I could feel the heat building in my hands, as if my fingers were swelling from the rage in my heart. "I don't know," I replied. "It's unreal."

"Let's go find out for sure then," Sharon said.

"But there's no way…" I insisted as I hurried to the driver's seat.

Speeding down Interstate Highway 76, I wondered if anything the woman said was true. I'd been Mrs. Bethanny Jean Everett for the past four years. Alexus and I dated my senior year in high school, and he proposed six months afterwards. He blamed his rush to get married on his plan to end his expensive tab at Roxy's strip club where I danced on weeknights. Alex, my top tipper, easily covered my eleven-hundred-dollar-a-month rent even though he didn't know it. I quit stripping after we got married when he begged me not to continue working there. He insisted he'd have to "kill" somebody for regarding his wife as a piece of meat.

"Come on, Bethanny," Sharon said. "We're here."

Opened the car door slowly, I walked through the stairway leading to Room 22. I knocked. After a few seconds, I knocked again, but somewhat harder. With still no answer, the two of us banged on the door again.

"Alex, I know you're in there!" I yelled. "Alex, how could you do this me? Why the lies, Alex?" Lifting my face away from the metal door, I found my brown makeup foundation smeared in the middle of the door. I heard whispers coming from behind the door, but couldn't make out what was being said.

After a few more minutes of banging, Sharon offered, "Let me bash the damn door open!" Pacing the balcony, Sharon looked under the banisters and around the cement, saying, "Where the hell is a rock when you need one?"

I shoved against the door and said, "Just be real, Alex."

Sharon went behind the bushes that were planted near the edge of the stairs and searched through the shrubs, "I can't find a rock, Bethanny," she said.

Wiped my tears with the back of my hand, I tapped my face on the center of the door, saying, "Be a man about it, and show your face."

"Don't cry, girl! If he's in there, he'll be crying tonight. Oh! I found one!" she exclaimed as she carried the baseball-sized gray stone up the steps.

A flashing police vehicle pulled into the parking lot, and she threw the rock onto the dirt. "Damn cops," Sharon mumbled.

"This is crazy; this is not real right now!" I told her.

"Calm down; it'll be all right," she said, patting my back, "You my sister, girl. I love you, honey. I'm here. That's what best friends is for."

Two Philadelphia police officers stepped out of the vehicle, and one held a flashlight in his hand.

"Ma'am, is there a problem?" the officer asked and I began to cry.

The middle-aged, heavy set police woman stood close to the police car and inspected the parked vehicles.

"Officer, she's just trying to locate her husband, that's all," Sharon said.

"Where is he?" the male officer asked. Hugging the side of his pistol like a cowboy in an old western film, his face was clean shaven, and his dark hair was neatly trimmed as he stared at us both.

"I think he's in room twenty-two," I said pointedly.

The male officer looked around the balcony of the motel, and pulled his flashlight into the corner of door to room number 22. He stepped in front of the door and knocked. "Police, open the door."

Alex opened the door and waved the officer in. His coffee-brown skin looked sweaty. He had a white towel wrapped over his head, and his black, wrinkled tee shirt disappeared back into the room.

"You're nothing but a pig!" Sharon yelled. "Just an old whore!"

"Let me see some identification, ma'am," the female officer said to Sharon, waving for me to come closer.

She told Sharon to quiet down before she began a line of questioning. "What's your husband's name?"

"Alexus Everett."

"What's your name?" The officer looked closely at the identification I handed her.

"Bethanny."

"Why are you here?"

I began to tell her about the troubles of the night.

"Who was the person that told you where to find him?"

"I don't know her, or her name." The officer looked suspiciously at me. "She called me about two hours ago. All she said was where they were."

"You can't come out here in the middle of the night, ma'am, and start banging on doors," the female officer said.

"I was told to."

"You can be arrested for trespassing,"

"We are good people, Officer. We weren't doing anything wrong, just trying to find her tired, trifling husband!" I rolled my eyes at Sharon. "I'm sorry," Sharon whispered.

"Well, ma'am, we've received numerous calls about a disturbance."

"From who? We just got here," I told her. I briefly wondered how I could kill Alex without any of them finding out.

"That's the law," the officer replied with a glare.

"I'm sorry, Officer,"

Sharon pulled my phone from my hands and pointed out the number of times the anonymous woman called. I couldn't compose myself any longer, and released blood-curdling screams I didn't know my lungs harbored. My screams came from the gut ugly pain that reeked inside my soul. However, they were cut short by Alex, who walked out of the motel room with a short, skinny, bronze-complected woman whose blonde hair cascaded in pristine condition despite their obvious indiscretion. The woman was shorter than the type of woman I envisioned Alex being attracted to, and she walked down the stairway in silence with only the sound of her red pumps clicking on the cement floor. Her black, zippered blouse exposed her bare back, which was decorated in an array of tattoos.

One stood out: *a rose with an arrow and a broken heart*. She pulled her miniskirt closer to her knees, and walked next to Alex as she passed by. I screamed until I felt my throat throbbing. "Whore!"

"You should be ashamed of yourself!" Sharon said, "He has children. *Children!* Do you not understand?" My legs finally gave out from under me, and I curled myself into a ball and simply sobbed.

"Get up, girl!" Sharon yelled. "Don't let them see you cry," she whispered as she pulled my arm and I pushed my body up from the ground.

The second officer accompanied the two to their vehicle. Husky, short and dark, Alex's buff body contrasted to my let-everything-go philosophy. He was very fit, and swore allegiance to the gym. His hairline was receding, however. I held my chest, coughing up anything I had in my throat, which I then hurled in Alex's direction. The two got into a red Mercedes and drove right past us.

"How could you do this to me, Alex?" I ran to his car, but the officer held me back.

"Take her home," the officer directed Sharon. I got into my car and ripped into my pocketbook, almost throwing everything in sight out onto the pavement.

"He's going to pay for this, Sharon," Sharon wrapped her arms around me and I rested my head on her shoulder. "I don't deserve this."

"No, you don't, sweetheart."

"It hurts. It really hurts," I cried.

"Yes, it does, sweetie. It's okay. Yes, it does."

CHAPTER 9 ANDRE

SCOOTER LEANED AGAINST THE brick wall of Brodie's corner store. Brodie's had been an intricate part of the South Philadelphia neighborhood for seventeen years. Only two blocks from Pastor's church, my sisters and I used to come every Sunday after church services for seventy-five-cent snacks. The place wasn't as well kept as it used to be. The bricks had crumbled and missing windows now dotted the side of the building. Brodie, who had to be in his seventies, opened the store later and closed it earlier these days.

Scooter's eyes moved like the hands on a grandfather clock. The sun's rays reflected his brown eyes. The hood of his sweatshirt covered his head as he pulled his beltless jeans higher up on his hips before dropping his bifocals onto the arch of his nose.

"Give me a quarter bag of white, Scooter," I said.

He eased closer to me before saying, "Got cash?"

Scooter was standing on the corner for a few hours before I could stomach even approaching him. I hadn't calmed down much since Cynthia pushed me to the limit like she did. I had to get something to settle my nerves and help me forget about what that girl may have had up her sleeve. Scooter just had to come through.

He and I went back, as in, way back, like the fourth grade. We shared classes together with my favorite math teacher, Mrs. Enrich. He always had a hard time staying seated, so she kept him in the corner of the classroom on those days when he couldn't sit still. I got Now and Later candies for treats while his treats were staring at the white corners of the room as I laughed along with the rest of the class. His speech wasn't the greatest either.

"Ee-igh-ty-fi-five dollars! You have it, you go—got it-it, man," Scooter stuttered, moving his long neck back and forth like an ostrich.

Scratching my sweaty hand, "Well, Scooter," I said.

Scooter was a hustler on the streets. I'd been putting him off, and asking for another IOU for the past two days, but I couldn't any longer. I shook nervously from the cold air. Licking my lips a couple times before I followed him, I bit my bottom lip. I waited a few seconds and hoped the silence sank in long enough for him to let me go on another pass.

"I need a hit."

But he didn't. "Pay up!" he demanded.

"I'm a little short today, Scooter man," I said. "I promise I'll have all your money in about a week."

"No, Andre," Scooter replied as he steadily shook his head. "You said that last week, Dre. T-t-tur-urn over eighty-five dollars," he repeated, "or you won't be getting a hit on me to-to-night." The veins on his temples stiffened as he added, "I can't keep looking out for y-y-ou, man. I-I'm coming up short, Andre."

Scooter took his glasses off his nose and rolled his crayon-brown eyes up as he pulled his glasses back onto his face, rubbing both hands together as if he were sanding wood. I wasn't sure I could convince him, but I figured I had to try. Digging into my blue jeans that I hadn't washed in more than a month, I pulled a partially disintegrated wad that was mixed with coins and held my hand out to Scooter.

"Man, that isn't enough!" Scooter said, examining my hands, "If it isn't eighty-five dollars, I-I-I don't want it. That is-isn't eighty-five dollars, man. Dre, beat it."

"Come on, Scooter, you know I'm good to pay you back," I said, hovering around him. "You know I'll pay you back." He moved about nervously, but I kept my eye on him. Scooter stood six feet tall and had deep dimples and thick eyebrows that rose above his glasses.

He regularly teased the pretty girls and bullied the nerds back in the day. He poked fun at anything he couldn't understand. We spent most of our days playing crap out in the school halls. He was the reason I had to repeat my senior year. His hair was individually braided and hung above his temple. He ran his tongue over his chipped tooth, but kept his eye on me. Huffing and puffing, he poked his chest out until it nearly touched mine and said, "Ma-ma-man, you know that's going to be one-one-one-one hundred and sixty-five dollars?"

I tabulated the latest total in my head. "Okay. Cool," I said, "I promise you, Scooter.

"Last time, Dre," he replied. "This is the las-la-last time." The tenor of his voice grew deeper. "The-the-this is the last time you owe me, man," he said. "If you don't have my money next week, I'll come collecting."

Scooter got to the edge of the curb and shook his head as he knelt down between two cinder blocks and retrieved a small plastic bag that held what I'd been craving all night. I'd just have to hustle a little more in order to repay him,

"I'm just waiting on my lady, Scooter man, waiting on Monique. She's going to get the rest of the money I stashed in the bank. She'll get it sometime tomorrow," I lied. I hadn't held a bank account for more than seven years. I couldn't manage to keep one with my wife, Monique, and me both pulling out money without checking beforehand with the other. Besides, no one would hire a three-time felon. Scooter's lips bunched together as he handed me the see-through bag of clumped white powder. I grabbed for it, and he held it a few seconds before releasing it to me.

"Don't make me have to send the goo-oo-ns out for you!" he warned. Scooter had threatened to unleash the goons on me at least three times before. I was still waiting for them.

"You won't need to, man, I got you covered!" I shot back. Scooter walked backwards, nearly bumping into a tall, skinny, toffee-skinned gentleman who waited at the side of the brick structure. Scooter's eyes fastened onto the man wearing a tan Timberland coat. His coat's brown neck trimming was also wrapped around his cuffs. His eyes were dark and his nose pointy. I stared at the familiar face.

"What up, Bruce?" Scooter said after shaking hands with the man. I gave Scooter a nod and made sure he was cool to be left alone. He nodded back.

"Thanks, Scooter," I said as I walked to my car that sat idling on the side of the street.

"How much did you get?" Shirley asked.

"Not enough for us both," I answered. Shirley was sprawled out on the passenger seat of my car. Her seat was reclined far enough to touch the rear seat.

"Oh? So you're not sharing?" she asked as she lifted herself from the seat.

"No, I can't," I said adamantly, looking back to where Scooter and the young man stood. "Where do I know that dude from?" I mumbled.

43

Scooter went back to the curb, bending under the cinder blocks while the man waited.

"What man?" Shirley asked. "Stop trying to change the subject, Andre; you're trying to be slick," she said as she rolled her eyes. "You're not going to pass some up?"

"No, seriously. That dude over there with Scooter," I pointed.

"Stop pointing!" Shirley swatted my finger away from the car window. "Let me have half of it," she demanded as she studied my jacket pocket.

"Now wait a minute, Shirley. I just paid for this stuff here, and I still owe him," I said.

"I gave you forty-five dollars," she said. "I'm tired of you doing this to me, Andre." I focused my eyes the road. "Give me back my money!" She smacked the side of my head and retreated to the corner of the passenger seat. I slammed my open hand on her back.

"Hey, now, don't get stupid," I chastised her.

I couldn't give her anything I didn't have, especially since Monique would certainly ask me for money as soon as I got in. Monique didn't go a day without asking for something. She didn't care where, or how I got it, but she always asked me for money, or just created something for me to do.

"I just paid Scooter with it. I don't have any money."

"Drop me off then," she said as she pulled her seat upright.

I pulled her arms to me. "Girl, you're not going anywhere," I shouted. Shirley moved her hand to the door handle, "Come on, baby. Oh, so now you want to leave me?" I whispered. I tried my sweet talk approach since it always worked before.

"That isn't right, Andre," she said as she rolled the green artificial contacts that kept her eyesight in check and kicked the floor mat. "That's cool though.".

Her mouth balled up like a fist. Her head was positioned at the passenger side window. I sped down the street, driving to the nearest corner and parked.

"Are you serious right now, baby?" I asked Shirley, who gathered her bags from under the seat. "I know you're not mad at me about that little bag he gave me. It's not enough, baby," I said. "It wouldn't even give you a buzz. Hell, it won't do much for me either." Shirley didn't respond. "So you're not speaking?" I took my left hand

and rubbed her right thigh. She flinched, then pushed me away. "Oh so that's how you treating me now?"

"Get off, Andre," she said as I squeezed her meaty thighs.

"I can't come tonight. My probation officer might sneak up on me since he's not been around in a week. I'll see you tomorrow." I puckered my lips and moved in to steal a kiss, saying, "Let me get some."

"No! "she said as she swung the door open before jumping out. "I can't help you if you're not looking out for me."

She slammed my blue Chevy metal door shut.

"Easy there, Shirley!" I yelled out my window. She moved ferociously down the street with legs shaped like a chicken's. Her butt cheeks moved up and down like a seesaw. She swung her head back toward me, and I blew her a kiss, but she flashed her left middle finger like a switchblade.

"I'll see you tomorrow, don't make me break that finger," I said. "All right, sweetheart?"

Shirley looked even prettier when she got angry. I wasn't one for running around with younger women, although I broke that rule when I began seeing Shirley, who was ten years my junior. When she started working at my parents' daycare center, I couldn't resist. By the time Ella, my older daughter, was attending the center, Shirley didn't hesitate to show me she was interested. She always smiled at me in the mornings, during drop-off. That young girl, innocent smile, as if I were the only one, the only king, who held, kissed, and sucked her the way she liked it best.

She licked her bottom lip while she spoke. Pink lips. With helium fullness and smooth as the moisture in her skin. Her contagious smile was a dead giveaway to her youth. We held full conversations when I picked Ella up in the afternoons. We spoke about sports, the foods she loved, the meals she cooked, which didn't help Monique, who hadn't cooked a soulful meal for me in a while. She blamed it on the kids making her too tired, but I think she's just lazy.

Shirley asked for a ride home one night after I picked Ella up. It was two minutes after closing, and she offered to waive the five-dollar-per-minute fee if I agreed to take her home after she cleaned up.

She kicked the toys to one side of the room, and shook out the

45

rugs before returning the kiddie chairs back to the desk. It took her all of five minutes to straighten up the cramped center. She locked up and even though I knew Pastor wouldn't charge the late fee, since I'd been late every day from the time Ella was enrolled, I played along and took the twenty-minute ride to her house with Ella in the back seat. Throughout the ride, she played with her curly hair. I watched her twist her blonde strands around her fingers and roll it over her lips as if she were directing me there. She gave me nothing but compliments about my skin tone, and how fit I looked. Shirley's long legs, round hips, and slender waistline made her what I considered nicely built. Fat failed to exist on her. She filled in all her curves proportionately. Her bronze skin and a ample chest, like two fat coconuts, were things Monique couldn't compare to. Within months after we hooked up, Pastor promoted her as his office secretary.

Shirley insisted her promotion had everything to do with our relationship, but I knew the truth. It was nothing but a coincidence. Pastor would never have approved of our affair even though Shirley didn't call it one. He may have had other things up his sleeve, but nothing like that. She said if a man wasn't sleeping in the same bedroom with his wife and stayed there only for the children, it wasn't an affair. I didn't disagree with her, although I didn't agree either.

Shirley and I pretty much did everything together. We smoked, drank good liquor and had good sex. In my car, in Pastor's office, and a few times on the mats of the church daycare center. She was more worried than I about getting caught. To help calm her nerves, I offered her a swig of white powder. She barked a lot when under stress, which was quite often. Within months, she stopped smoking weed, and we just snorted exclusively.

CHAPTER 10 Pharah

SITTING ON THE STEPS that led into the church's basement, I counted the folded tables that Raymond, one of our male choir members, was kind enough to park across from me, although he had to leave work to do it. Twenty-four, twenty-eight, and that made thirty tables. Just enough for the two hundred and eleven invited wedding guests. The sky blue walls could have used a fresh coat of paint, but Momma didn't include that in her budget. I, for sure, would never have held my special day in a dark, gloomy basement, but I intended to make it work out for Naomi and her fiancé.

I checked my wristwatch for the first time since I began waiting for the deejay. I'd been there thirty minutes, and judging by the looks of it, he was late. My profile for the Christian Mingle account should have gone live fully this afternoon. I planned to return to my apartment in forty-five minutes, which could have been a problem if this guy didn't get here soon. Feeling both optimistic and nervous about it, I flicked through my cell phone to see if there was any sign of life in my dating file.

Singling out one of two best pictures of my half smile, I chose the one that revealed just enough teeth to let you know I at least had some.

"I'm so sorry I'm late," said the six-foot-something male as he barged down the stairway. I stepped up to reach for his hand. Curly, black, frizzy hair, and a mustache comprised his dapper facial hair. The red flannel shirt he was wearing was a size too small, and his jeans were rolled up at the ankles.

The palms of my hand felt sticky, so I wiped them on the side of my blue jeans and offered him my other one.

"Pharah," I said, "God bless you. It's very nice to meet you."

Quite an entrance for an albino with a gap between his front teeth. I wondered how many times he'd been teased.

"Stuck in traffic," he said, adding, "I hope you didn't wait too long?"

Thirty-one minutes and counting, but I wouldn't hold that against him. His hands weren't soft, but they were firm. His lips were dry, but nothing Vaseline couldn't fix.

"No, don't worry. *You're fine*," I said.

"I'm Jeremy," he said, "but just call me Beats."

I watched the way the upper part of his lip sucked in after each word he said, as if the hole between his teeth was big enough to store it. His arms were as buff as my bedroom pillows.

"Nice."

I waved for him to sit down so he wouldn't feel as awkward as I did when someone stared too long. *Are they looking at my tooth? Or my kinky hair?* I patted my hair.

"I need a deejay," I said. In the gloomiest part of my mind, I recited, *I NEED A MAN*, before walking over to the empty folding chair. I sat down in it to face him.

"I'm your guy," he said, fully revealing the gap in his teeth. To avoid letting my eyes wander to it, I looked inside my folder for direction.

"Thee guy, huh?" I said. Shuffling through the folder, I searched for the list of questions I previously prepared to ask him. The dead silence made it difficult not to wonder if he was looking for something of value in me.

"How long have you been a deejay?" I said, tossing the folder on the table and turning my attention back to him.

"It's been about five years," he said. "I do weddings, parties, funerals."

I let him go on telling me about himself, and nodded a few times to reassure him that I was all ears.

"I have everything you'll need," he said. He pulled his backpack on the table and shuffled through the pile of CDs stacked in the small bag. He popped one into his portable CD player.

"I have Faith Hill, Boys to Men, and…"

"No, we won't need those," I said. "This is a church wedding. All you'll need is the equipment. Most of the songs have already been pre-selected. The bride has made a specific request for one melody, but I'll get that to you right before the wedding. I'll also provide you with a list of when to play the selected songs."

Beats' eyebrows rose and he scratched his face while opening his mouth to speak, but he didn't.

"You're hired, if you can get here on time."

I chewed on my cheek, and looked at my watch. Only nineteen minutes before my site went live. "Can you do that?" I asked.

He gave me a suspicious-looking expression that even gave his pale skin some color.

"That's cool," he said, "but I like to play my own stuff." He remained motionless, but appeared bothered. "It's for a wedding right the way through?"

"Yes."

"That's odd; most weddings I deejay don't really give me any particular music. I just bring my own," he said.

I gave him another second to decide where he was going with his comment, since my offer was the only one on the table. I reached for my folder and gave his gap a few more seconds of my time before saying, "Crieur family weddings are much different."

CHAPTER 11 Cynthia

I KNEW IF I STOPPED, SOMEHOW OR another, I'd be badgered with questions. And I was right.

"What are you doing here?" James asked. "Working, huh?"

His chalk-white teeth were straight behind his full lips. He looked me up and down as if I were an edible bikini model. James lived in our old neighborhood on Tyler street, and was known as being most popular. He had plenty of teenage girls interested in his athletic abilities.

Muscular by nature, might have been enough to keep most girls intrigued, but he didn't do much for me. That was one of the reasons we got along as well as we did in high school. I knew him for who he was: slick, arrogant and horny.

"I heard you're a lawyer now," he said.

"Yes," I replied. "I graduated from law school, Rutgers University, last year."

"Wow," he said, "not too shabby, Shorty. I knew you'd be somebody one day."

I winked at him because I did too.

"Rogers graduate, huh?"

"Rutgers, Rutgers," I repeated. "RUT-GERS."

"Oh. I guess that's why you don't recognize me now," he said, brandishing his deep dimples. They weren't as impressive, however, as a college degree.

"You've lost some weight, I see," I said.

"Yeah haven't been going to the gym like I used to," he answered, "but I still have some irons right here though." Pointing to his abs, he added, "Guess that's why you fronting on me now."

The line across his belly was as crisply defined as his rippled skin. The firmness of his bare skin held up while he balled the ends of his shirt in his hand.

"No," I said, "never," biting the skin of my lips. "So how have you been?" I said to change the subject.

"I've been pretty good, just got into a little trouble, but came home a few months ago," he answered.

"Home from where?"

"Jail," he said. "Cynthia, has law school wiped out all your street vocabulary?" His casual laughter was unassuming, but the street language wasn't impressive. Speak properly and act properly too.

"Just proper English," I said, avoiding his humor over it altogether.

"Street language is in my blood," he said, "so I don't know. it's my English." He lay his shirt back on his abs and his posture turned serious. I crossed my arms. He seemed unmoved by my silence.

"I see your body's nice and built, and got even thicker," he said.

"Well, nothing as good as me ever really changes, honey," I replied. He laughed, and I couldn't help joining.

"You're probably right about that," he said.

"Oh, I am," I agreed, "trust me. Confidence always wins even without any effort."

James's eyes fastened onto mine like he were trying to find a soft spot. Or looking to crack open a safe. I did just as he did, but I wasn't looking to solve a mystery.

"Why were you incarcerated?" I inquired, "if you don't mind me asking."

He looked around the parking lot, then rested his arm on the roof of his car. "Well, you know, I was doing some things."

"Things? Like what?" I asked.

"What are you? A cop?" James replied sarcastically.

"No, but I would like to know. It's not classified information, is it?" I shrugged. His business was simply for my information. It wasn't like his story would have been any different from my other clients. They robbed banks, stores, homes; nothing was ever off limits.

"I got mixed up with the wrong crowd, you know how that goes."

"Oh, the same sob story, huh?" I said instinctively.

"It's not a sob story, *Cynthia*." He whispered my name as if disappointed by my response.

"So are you taking care of yourself now? Are you behaving?"

I diverted my line of questioning in order to avoid reducing him anymore than I may have already.

"Yes. I am, Cynthia, I have to."

"Well? What are you doing? Do you have a job?"

James's lips moved, but I couldn't hear so I moved closer to where he stood.

"Got a job at the supermarket," he said, "Waiting on a call back from another job I really want. Got to stay busy, you know. I come by here at three o'clock every Friday to meet with my P.O. I mean, my probation officer."

"Do you have any career plans? To earn more money?"

"I'm working on it."

"Working on it? How long have you been out of jail?" I asked.

He wrinkled his eyebrows. "It's hard out here for someone like me."

I clapped my hands to every word he said and replied, "Excuses, excuses, excuses." He stood there mute. I waited for him to throw out some nasty slur, or dig, to set me straight. My job helped me be prepared for it. It wouldn't have been the first time I heard such criticism so I fully expected him to reply in anger. "If you truly wanted a job, you'd find one."

"I'm trying," James said. "I'm trying to do whatever I can for my kids."

"Kids?" I repeated, leaving no room for the possibility of skepticism. "You brought kids into this mess too?" James still hadn't moved an inch. He stood with a perplexed stare for a few seconds before exploding into laughter.

"What do you mean?" he asked.

"I mean, if your life isn't right, why subject innocent children to it?" I said. "Couldn't you be more responsible?"

He slowly backed away from me. "Hey," he said, "I've made poor choices, but I wouldn't change having my girls." Those white teeth gleamed as he relaxed his shoulders and confessed. "I love them girls," he finished.

"Good," I said. I felt the urge to give my advice on contraceptives, but let that go,

"Well, that's good to hear," I said, looking around for my car.

"Just because I committed a crime doesn't make me a criminal," he said. "I simply committed a crime. I don't confuse the two."

"Oh, really?" I said, laughing at the seriousness in his face. "I beg to differ."

James's eyes were hollow. Just as empty as his analogies. I shook my head before leaning against James's car and waited to hear his speech about redemption.

"It was nice seeing you," he said, abruptly pulled his car door open before approaching me for a hug.

Taken aback by his sudden, hasty departure, I inexplicably said, "Why don't I call you sometime?"

His head hung low, but not nearly as low as my dignity dropped. He stood motionless. "Are you sure about that?" he asked in a whisper.

I battered my eyes, either because of my nerves or my anger. "I'm not begging you," I said, digging into my purse for my cell phone. "What's the number?" I held the phone in my hand and waited for a reaction, but he wouldn't budge.

"I'll take yours instead," he said, jamming his hand into his pants pocket like he just checkmated. So, instead of storming away, as I would have done with other vagrants, I did the unthinkable. I spilled all ten numerical digits to my cell phone without a single moment of hesitation.

My period wasn't on, so I was not acting out of emotion. I had only a single cup of coffee today. *Why in the world did I give this man my real phone number?*

"All right then," he said as he wrapped his thin arms around my neck. I gently hugged him back, slightly unsure of what just happened. He hopped into his car and sped away.

After I started my car, I checked myself in the driver's mirror. *Who are you?* My eye was still puffy so I dabbed it a few times. *James Ingrid.* I gave James Ingrid my phone number without him begging me for it. He wouldn't have the nerve to call. I was tired and drained by all of the drama in my life. He probably recognized my temporary weakness and decided to go for it. Just like any felon who commits crimes. This was a crime of opportunity. He's the kind who would be callous to his victims, too; and dishonest in his surroundings, including everyone he meets.

I was coming out of a courthouse, and for all he knew, I'd been in there all day. No cause for irrational behavior. But he managed to do that? To manipulate me into giving him my personal number?

"Agh!" I grumbled before driving off.

CHAPTER 12 Naomi

INSTEAD OF SCREAMING *BLOODY MARY* TO MOMMA, who stood in front of the stove with her back to me, I stood at the doorway of the kitchen and waited for her speak.

"Are you going to eat, honey?" Momma asked. She lifted the cover of the pot to reveal what I'd been missing out on for the past few months. Her robe was the same as it was every day: cotton, blue and big. Her eyes widened in her round, licorice-black, sweaty face.

"I'll eat," I said even though I wasn't hungry.

"You are supposed to feed the baby," she said. "I don't know why you young PEE-POLE decides to have kids if you don't know what to do."

Momma was in her "let's bash young people" mood again. She would not find one good thing to say about them for the next few hours. That's usually how long it took her to notice she was beating a dead horse. I wouldn't actually disagree, but I did my usual and whispered in my head, *Why don't old people stop thinking they're right all the time?*

Try to envision me sticking my tongue out with my fingers drilled in each ear, wiggling at the stupidity and annoyance of her unwanted comments. Comments that invariably reminded me why I didn't miss living with her. Or the calls in the middle of the night from her to "come down and braid my hair," or "wash the dishes, Naomi," or "eat!" or "yes, you are going to church." She never asked me, she only told me what to do. Our house was perpetually full of visitors who always came empty-handed. Momma fed everyone on Sundays.

Every Sunday morning, just before getting ready for church, Momma got up by six a.m. to start Sunday's dinner. You could hear her in the kitchen, praying, while everyone else (like me) tried to get a bit more sleep. That put a lot of pressure on me as the youngest, especially since Pastor's motto was methodically drilled into my skull: "Do whatever you're told so you won't end up like the others."

Those words will forever be engraved in my head.

I knew what he meant by the *other*s: Andre, Bethanny and Rachel, the *sinners,* as Pastor referred to them. The ones who took a chance and did what they wanted, not what my parents dictated for them. They took the chance I was not confident enough to take. Odds were, my choices were doomed from the very start. Their usually ill-fated disasters were planned *for* me, not *by* me, including my upcoming nuptials.

Mom's check-list for me: Never fuss. Pretend everything she and Pastor ever told me *must be* true, in *Jesus's name*.

Dad's check-list for me: If you don't do what you're told, you'll be disowned.

I was their last child, so I did what I was told for the most part. The third daughter of Pastor was in jeopardy of being blacklisted from his love. There were strict rules to abide by, the Crieur girls' rules:

no worldly activities or movies.

no hanging out with friends.

no overnight stays at friends'.

no sleepovers at my house.

no cable TV.

no extra-curricular activity if it does not include the church family.

There were plenty of yeses too. Like saying yes to chores, and yes to going to church, and absolutely yes to maintaining a clean house.

"Drink," Momma ordered. She placed the cup of tea in front of me and stood with her long spoon at the foot of the table.

"Yes, Momma," I said. "Thanks." I was careful not to stare at her for too long so she wouldn't start again.

"You need all the vitamins you can get. That baby is taking away all your nutrients, and unless you're eating right, he won't be as strong," Momma said in her authoritative voice that always drowned out whatever I was thinking.

"Okay," I said, "and SHE is going to be strong."

I held the top of the chair to reassure Momma I was being a good listener; but Jessa started kicking again, in objection, I suppose.

"Don't stand there!" she said. "Sit down, Naomi."

"I'd rather stand, Momma," I said.

She jerked her head around to look to me and rolled her eyes. I squeezed my hand around my waist. The smell of Momma's kale tea filled the room.

"Just for a second, okay? My side hurts," I explained. I pulled the wooden chair out from under the table, then sat.

"A pregnant woman doesn't stand on her feet for long; it's not good for the baby," she muttered, pouting her lips in contrast to my welcome smile.

"I'm beginning to think the wedding is costing too much," I said, "so let's push back the date."

Jessa started kicking again, so I wrapped my hand around my belly and wished I could do the same around Momma's lips.

"No," she said, "you should be planning the wedding now. Wouldn't you prefer to bring the baby into this world legitimately, Naomi?"

Momma's worried look demanded a response. "You're right, Momma," I said, taking a sip from the tea. She scurried back to the stove, stirring whatever she had cooking before slamming the spoon on top of the stove. Then she turned to face me.

"You can't keep embarrassing yourself like this, young lady," Momma chided. That was the other annoying introduction to her conservative proclamation.

"Mom," I said, "it doesn't make any difference, really."

"Of course, it makes a difference!" she insisted. "How does that look to the church? The least you can do is marry the man who is shaming you."

And the ball dropped again. The litany of Momma Crieur's rules, just itching to surface.

"All right mother," I obediently replied. The flutters from Jessa stopped, but now my chest hurt. Momma's dark eyes never left mine. Her four-foot height did nothing to diminish her tall orders.

I picked at the food on my plate. Momma placed a second cup of tea next to it and the steam from the cup evaporated as quickly as the feeling of peace left the room.

"Drink it," she ordered, but I hesitated in protest. The peace in me eventually was squeezed out.

"I don't want it, "I said in a whisper and low enough that she couldn't hear.

"Drink it, all of it too," she said, pushing the mug in front of me.

I held the mug handle.

"What time does Norman get off work?" she asked. I wasn't prepared for a fight. Never had been.

"In a few hours, Momma," I replied, "so I should get ready to go."

"Have you started buying things for the baby?" she asked. "I told you to buy some undershirts over at Babies R Us while they're still on sale."

I wanted to scream *the money isn't there!* but she said, "Did you buy them yet?"

"No," I said. "I found cheaper ones at Value City, and picked up a few there."

The disgust in her eyes was visible. "Naomi, I want you to try on your dress here later on this week so I can take a look at you in it. I don't want you coming to the church with a big, ol' belly dress. Can't wait until he makes you a legitimate woman," she said, shaking her head.

"I am a legitimate woman," I countered, looking down at the mug and ready to flash my driver's license before demanding that she recognize my legal age. The ensuing silence made me steal a quick glance at her.

Momma raised her head and said, "A legitimate woman huh?" Then I turned away, unfazed by the fire I just ignited.

"Well, are you already married?" she asked. I responded in the way that I knew was best. I did what I'd done for as many years as Momma has won her arguments. I shut down. Sucked in my pride, my urge to respond to her barbs was all wrapped up and carefully stashed into one huge hole.

"I was just kidding, Momma," I said as I plastered my usual, fake smile back on.

CHAPTER 13 Andre

I DROVE TWO STREETS DOWN before parking along the row of houses. All of them looked the same. Maroon bricks and straw lawn sets filled the porches of the homes. Wind chimes tinkled in the light wind from the end-of-summer breeze. I opened my brown coat and pulled out a pipe that I'd rigged up. I smacked it a few times, being careful not to disturb the clear sealing tape that held it together. I poured the contents of the baggie into the bowl, and slipped my hand into my pocket to get out my lighter before lighting the end of the pipe. The car quickly filled up with a cloud of gray smoke and I blew the hit out of my mouth. I leaned my head against the headrest and closed my eyes before taking another puff. I thought about paying Momma a visit.

I hadn't been back to Momma's house since my encounter with Cynthia. But I didn't like visiting her when I was feeling this good. Not as quick on my toes, she'd, no doubt, blow my high. I pulled my phone out of my back pocket and checked my voicemail for messages. Momma called three times. She left a message that said: *"You want to go to jail, right? Well, you'll go right back there if Cynthia presses charges. You ain't no good; never have been, and never will be. Acting like an animal,"* she said, *"you need to get to church. Ask the dear Lord to give you some sense. Did you get your tux?"*

I figured after a few days, she'd stop bothering me about Cynthia, and certainly by now. Her nagging wouldn't stop, however. She'd eventually bug me some more about Naomi's wedding too. I didn't see the point. I didn't have any money and I couldn't go back to jail. Besides, whenever we all got together, I found myself growing defensive and feeling the need to rationalize my existence to my lame, little sisters. I've got enough going on with my probation officer who's giving me hell about staying out of trouble. To make matters worse, the judge ordered probation for two whole years.

When I heard the ruling, everything in the courtroom looked small to me. My mother's hat, the guard, and even me. The room smelled like burning charcoal. Sawdust filled the air. I can't go back to jail, but it isn't easy staying out of trouble. I nearly passed out in the middle of the floor of the filled courtroom. You'd think that having a sister as a lawyer might permanently end my legal problems. But she always acts as if she's too good to help me remain free. I'm struggling, but she doesn't care. My lawyer seems to think Monique's letter to the judge about our kids might've lessened the sentence. I don't think it's a lesser anything because I'm still confined, trapped and limited to whatever they tell me to do.

Like the time Momma sent Bethanny and me to live with her sisters in Georgia. The smell of red java beans being cooked in a silver pot still lingers in the memory of my mind. The silver pot shone on the burner as brightly as Pastor's caps on his front teeth. I remembered standing on a wood bench with my Auntie Rashi's sugar cane stick to spin the beans in the pot. Water billowed out of the pot like a volcanic eruption, which became a source of fear for me as a five-year-old. I worried about being swallowed by the boiling hot water. I didn't resent my parents for leaving us to start their *ministry,* as they called it. Not even for changing our last names from Grimes to Crieur, since Pastor thought his ministry needed a "fresh start." It was the "only way" they said they could help Bethanny and me.

They didn't mind stepping all over us to get where they had to go, but at least, they threw me a rope when they made it. With three hundred members in their church and Pastor collecting monthly payroll checks from it, I couldn't get mad at them now. I often tell Bethanny how their efforts saved us, but she doesn't buy it.

She just pulls her pant leg up again and shows me the buckle burns Auntie Rashi left on her rustic brown skin. "They left us because they wanted us to get beaten," she'd always say about Momma and Pastor.

By the time they returned for us, we were almost pre-teens. I already had my mind made up as to who I was and who I wanted to be. Although, it was like living with strangers, I no longer knew who my parents were. I went to school, and did as I was told, helping with my younger siblings, but over the years, I asked to do more outside the home. Pastor, however, didn't agree. The more he didn't listen to me, the more I stopped listening to him. By the time I was sixteen, Pastor was growing frustrated with five kids running around the house. So much so, he slapped Momma very hard one day, so hard, I dropped my dinner plate right on the floor. Momma turned her left cheek and spoke in a sweet, calm voice, "Give me one there too."

I was angry, and I jumped on Pastor's back. I punched, kicked and yelled. "Don't you ever touch my mother again," I warned him.
He yanked my shoulders and tried to stop my incessant blows. It didn't work. He seldom spoke to me after that. Not even fifteen years later.

"Your mother called again," Monique announced as I stepped inside our apartment. She stood in the doorway with her hand on her hip.

"Daddy!" my two little girls, Emily and Ella, exclaimed as they jumped off the sofa and ran over to me. I took a long drag off my cigarette before offering it to Monique. She ran her hands over the center of her round belly, and placed each hand on the sides of her waist before rubbing her belly softly over her dress. I moved my fingers to the middle of her stomach, and kissed it before I let go.

"Is he kicking?" I asked.

"No," Monique replied, "not as much today."

"Hey, precious," I said, lifting my two girls, one in each arm. Each child wore pigtails with barrettes dangling from their braids.

"Where have you been, Daddy?"

"Well, Ella," I said, "Daddy's been working." I kissed her cheek before taking a seat on the maroon sofa and putting the two girls on my lap. Ella grinned. Her top two teeth were missing, and her skin was as pale as her mother's. Emily's was ebony-black like my mother. An inch taller than her little sister, her big brown eyes curiously rested on me. Monique sat across from me, wagging her leg.

"What'd she say?" I asked.

"She said something about making sure you had your suit. I couldn't understand what she said." Monique held the cigarette in the corner of her mouth and fanned the cloud of smoke around her.

"Oh yeah," I said, "I forgot. I was supposed to meet up with Pharah."

"For what?" Monique asked, her chin wrinkling.

"Supposed to get my tuxedo or something," I said. "I haven't done any shopping yet." Monique punched the butt of her cigarette into the silver ashtray that sat on the edge of the coffee table.

"We haven't gotten either of the girls' dresses," she reminded me. "We need some money."

"I know," I said. "We'll figure it out."

"Will you?" she said, looking at me from the corner of her right eye.

She was right. I still didn't know where I'd get Scooter's cash, and more cash for more white.

"Got a lot on our plate right now," she said, "and as for me, the most important thing is your freedom. You don't know how important your freedom is. It's much more important than any other nonsense that's happening right now."

"Who you telling?"

Monique motioned for me to "Shh!" The reaction from the five-eleven, high-pitched pregnant woman's voice suggested her patience was wearing thin. But so was mine.

"What do you want me to do?" I asked, "rob a bank?"

"If you're not here for your sister's wedding, then what?" The redness in Monique's cheeks grew darker.

I already had it out with Shirley today, and didn't want Monique on my list too. That was just too much for one night.

Monique crossed her spaghetti noodle legs in her seat and rubbed her stomach.

"Are you going back to Leroy's house tonight?" she asked. Leroy was a code word for Shirley. But Monique hadn't caught on to that yet.

"Chilling with the family tonight," I said. Shirley wouldn't take kindly to me staying away for more than one night. I managed to accommodate her for as long as my probation officer changed my home visits from four nights to two nights per month.

"Didn't you say I haven't been spending enough time with you?" I was responding to the many evil glares and tongue lashings I'd been receiving for the past seven years. No doubt, I've given her plenty of reasons to be suspicious, but I'd been real good at keeping things from her lately. Better than I thought I was. Besides, our union was doomed from the very beginning.

I call our matrimony the tragic consequence of a drunken night at a downtown bar. By the time I got tired of rolling around with Monique, she was already pregnant. Momma said, like many

First Ladies of a Baptist church, *"You're marrying her,"* and I did, but only two years after our second child was born.

"Yeah," she said, "you've been uptight though. The judge won't send you to jail if you've been good." She lit another cigarette, inhaled for a few seconds, then let it out her nostrils.

"Yeah," I said, "playing it safe. Right, girls?"

Ella was playing a game of peek-a-boo with me, and I pinched her rosy cheeks.

"I spoke to the lawyer this morning," she said. "Judge can change his mind anytime."

"Look, Monique, let's talk about something else," I said, seeking an escape from this never-ending discussion. "Baby, I just want to be where my babies are. That's all I care about right now; that's all. Just being with my babies."

"I don't know, Andre. Suppose you can't find a job and the judge doesn't think you're doing everything you should for your family?" she asked, "then what, Andre?"

Monique stood between the door and the couch, tapping her heels on the hardwood floor.

"They won't," I said "Damn! Let's drop it already."

Irritated by worry, and angered by the lack of control of my own demise, I watched as Ella hopped off my lap, and Emily plugged her thumb in her mouth. I scooted her off my lap and kissed her forehead before going up the stairs.

"Where are you going, Daddy?" Ella asked.

"I'll be right back, baby," I said.

Going into my bedroom closet, I shook a couple of Monique's handbags for anything I could sell. I climbed on top of Monique's shoeboxes and reached for the New King James Bible. Placing the Bible on top of the lion print quilt on the bed, I shuffled through my jacket pocket and pulled out the remainder of white. Opening the good book, I looked around the room before sliding my hand in the hole I carved, about the size of a mug, and I jerked the metal pipe from my pocket. Quickly lighting it, I inhaled a few puffs before returning it to its rightful place. I slapped my jeans to discard all evidence of my actions, and strolled out into the hall and rubbed my stomach. "Monique," I said, "you have anything down there to eat? Daddy's hungry."

Chapter 14 Bethanny

I STOOD AT THE ELEVATOR DOOR in the lobby of Alex's work and waited an hour before I was told by the security officers that Alex did not want to see me.

"I'm not leaving unless he does," I said adamantly, angered by his cavalier attitude. I followed my disgust with two text messages that I sent while I waited,

IM NOT LEAVING. YOU NEED TO GET DOWN HERE NOW.

He responded: *I DON'T WANT YOU HERE JUST LEAVE ME ALONE!*

I decided not to. By the time the third officer approached, I pushed my double Ds closer to the top of my bra. Then I took the blue sweater I had wrapped around my waist and flung it on top of the security officer's desk. I decided to let my bust determine whether or not the officers would bring Alex to me.

Once Alex arrived, we stood near one another like strangers. I remained firm. "You need to come home."

"Why are you here?" he asked.

His hair hasn't been combed in days and his beard was bushy and untrimmed. His shirt wasn't ironed. Obviously, his new partner wasn't delivering in her new title. Strange how our roles suddenly reversed! He used to compliment how well I took extra care with his things. And how I attended to all of his needs.

The elevator door closed behind him and the officers huddled together in the middle of the patrol area. Eye gawkers rested their gazes on my bare legs as whispers of our marital bliss could be heard in the lobby, while the smell of lust billowed nearby.

"We need to talk, Alex." He lifted his hand over his face. *No wedding ring?* Apparently, I'd already been replaced.

"This is too much," he said "We don't need to talk. I'll have the rest of my things out of the house within a week."

"You can't do this!" My heart fluttered mid-sentence before I added, "Are you giving up on us? On our family?"

"Family?" Alex said the word as if it were foreign to his tongue. The long, white dress I purchased for five hundred dollars at

David's Bridal still hung in my closet, safely stored away for my own daughter's nuptials.

"I'm not talking about this right now," he said.

"When can we talk about it?" I asked. Searching my mind for questions to keep him near, I said, "You don't come home anymore. You're not answering my calls. What have I done to you, Alex?" I pleaded, hoping he could hear the fear festering inside. "I've been nothing but a good wife to you," I continued. "A good mother to your children. You haven't even called…"

"I don't want to do this here," he said.

"Then where shall we do it?" I asked sarcastically, resting my hands on my hips. Alex did a weird thing with his face again, making an expression like you might make if you were trapped in a room of smelly people. He screwed up his face and fanned the air around me, as if I were the culprit.

",No," he said. "We're not getting back together."

"Why not?"

"I'm happy where I am," he replied, and his words stung me to the core. I was once his happiness. He wrote his own wedding vows and called me his "happiness."

"What?" I protested. "I loved you exclusively for seven years of my life. How can you so easily break my heart?"

"Shh!" he said, "It hasn't been working out, Bethanny." I only wished he could've let me in on the news earlier. I would have been better prepared. He kept coming home to me without showing any signs of being unsure. Even the mean faces he periodically displayed in the past led me to believe he was simply tired. There were no doubts of his fidelity in my mind.

"How?"

"You're not the woman I married," he said, then added as if to explain, "you're always bitter and hateful."

I cringed at words he used since they were the same ones I used to question him when he lay stiffly in bed after I shared my day and anecdotes about the kids. I remembered often asking if something I said bothered him, but he always denied it.

"You sit around complaining about everything!" he said. "I could buy you the whole world and you'd still be unhappy."

I pretended his words didn't hit the very heart of my soul. Tiny drops of his spit popped on my cheek from the simmering rage that escaped from his lips.

"I've begged you to communicate with me. And leave all your issues with your family out of it," he said. "To love me like I loved you. And show me how you care instead of being such a robot, with no emotion and making your beef with your family my problem."

Who else was I to discuss my family issues with? My depressive symptom, when I didn't want to get out of bed and face the world, overcame me more times than I could count. I laid my feelings on the line and hoped he'd understand me better, and why I couldn't always welcome his hugs and spontaneous kisses. Something inside me made me feel I didn't deserve it.

"I'm done," he said.

I searched for a word, or a thought, or a memory, an ounce of anything I could send his way just so he could throw me a life jacket. "I'm sorry," I said.

"How do you think I feel having to tiptoe around you and your family?" he asked. He deliberately ignored the sincerity of my existence. "I wasn't raised liked that," he continued. "My mother didn't teach me to make enemies with the very people you're supposed to love. No. You taught me that."

I waited for his facial veins to move back into place before I considered my response.

"I'm not pretending anymore," he said. "You come down here wearing a mini skirt like you want to perform for these people."

The thought of excusing myself to take possession of my sweater briefly crossed my mind. but I decided against it. "I've never put you in the middle of anything," I argued. "I've simply confided in you."

"And I've confided in you," he said. "My mother welcomed you, and my family. But that wasn't good enough. You want me to showboat at your sister's wedding, only to bash me later about how much fun I had mingling with them. I can't do anything right in your eyes."

His eyes suddenly widened, and I looked away. I wouldn't have been angry if he mingled. Only if he discussed our personal lives with the people he mingled with. It's no secret that I'm not one of my parents' "greatest assets" and I certainly don't consider them any of mine.

Alex could scream as much as he wanted about being "raised by a wonderful, old woman, whom he kept at his disposal, and she was always his because she loved him;" but when would he try to understand my issues? Weren't my repeated efforts to "shush" him when he gloated about our finances enough of a warning? I caught the glances of the security officers who pretended as if I hadn't seen them.

"You want attention, right?" he said, "well, there you have it!" Alex backed away from me and smacked the elevator button.

"I've supported you, Alex," I said. "I shared what bothers me with you. I had no intentions of ever hurting you."

"Doesn't matter," he said. At this moment, he was right: it didn't matter. I was not ready to be alone, although for the past seventeen years, I guess I was. Spilling my guts into my diary didn't diminish the loneliness. Neither did sharing my bed nor my marriage.

"Whether you intended for it to happen or not, it's not working for me," he said.

"You've left me without any money," I said, trying another approach to keep him there. "There's nothing to feed the kids, Alex."

Alex turned and gave me the *you smell* look again. "You know good and well you've taken money from my account!" he said.

We did. Sharon and I stopped at three different ATM machines that fateful night. We withdrew three hundred from our joint account, and five hundred from Alex's credit card, which depleted his savings.

"What did you want me to do, Alex?" I sighed. "You left us for some two-dollar trick!"

"Isn't that what it cost when I got you?" he said sadistically. Seeing the fire in his eyes, I pretended I didn't hear him. The two dollars multiply quickly when you swirl around a pole naked at a bar of chanting men. Alex was one of them.

I said, "What do you expect us to live on?"

"Quiet down!" He pulled me by the wrist, closer to his chest, "I'm going to put a few dollars into your account," he said. "Don't come back here."

Using my chest as if it were my hand, I pushed him away. His surrender to my argument wasn't the way I envisioned it.

"Get out of my face!" I said. "You're worried about these people?" I pointed to the eyes and ears trafficking the halls, as well as the suits that stood in front of the elevator and the uniforms walking by.

"Wait until I talk to your mother!" I said, aware his schoolboy innocence would crumble, just like my marriage. His greatest accomplishment besides his children was marrying me.

"Well, what about your family, Alex?" I said, "and your children?"

My voice echoed beyond the confines of the lobby, attracting more wandering eyes and attentive ears.

"If you are not going to talk to me, Alex, at least, have the decency to tell me why?" I demanded.

"I just did," he whispered.

"That's not why," I said. "You're turning this whole indiscretion around on me." Suddenly, the reality of my situation began setting in. "You've wronged me!"

"Stay away from here!" he said. "Call whoever you want. I'm done." Clenching his fists by his sides, he stepped inside the elevator.

"Be responsible for your family, Alex!" I shouted. "Don't do this to our family!"

Pleading is equal to begging, and that's something I'm rather good at. But with Alex, the more I spoke, the less he did, so I said as much as I could in the short window I was given.

"You keep pushing," he said, "and I'll have my attorney file for full custody of my kids."

I slammed my hands on the doors of the elevator and kicked my foot in between to keep the elevator door open. There wasn't anything or anyone that could have kept me away from my kids. I hadn't worked in six years just so I could stay home with them.

"Full custody?"

"Yes," he said. "*Full custody* of my children, you can't take care of them without me. You can barely care for yourself." He had an ugly, smug smile on his face.

"Why are you doing this to me?" I asked, raising my hand to strike a blow, but dropping the idea once I thought of the consequences. "Not my kids!"

"Get back, Bethanny," Alex said, his voice growing weaker and less convincing as he stepped into the elevator. "You're doing way too much right now." He pushed his forearm in my middle area and said, "It's over."

"Your whore won't raise my kids!" I spat. "Not in this lifetime!" I waved my hand in the air to let him know he hadn't conquered me. However, an overwhelming sense of defeat hovered over my shoulder. He was gone forever. The kids wouldn't be raised by two parents. They'd feel the same abandonment my parents dropped on me.

"Tell these people where you've been?" I said, allowing the rage inside me to fester no more. A tap from behind just sent me screaming louder. "Tell these people what you've been up to, Alex!" I insisted.

A soft whisper in my ear said, "Quiet down. It's all right." The voice came from a pale man with a thousand keys wrapped around his belt. He was dressed in the same uniform I ironed each week for Alex, so I looked to him for support.

"I'm his wife," I said, "what have I done to deserve this?"

"This is neither the time, nor the place for this conversation," the pale man said. "I'm afraid I have to ask you to leave."

By the time I turned away from pale man, Alex had already disappeared. My heart refused to let him go. The memories of times when we were happy danced around in my head. The ping from the elevator and the sound of the automatic door sliding open and shut exaggerated the numbness I felt.

"I've taken care of his children," I whined, "and taken care of him! And this is how he thanks me?" I held the pale man by his elbow and hoped he'd hold me up if my legs gave way again. "He's cheating on me and said he's leaving me," I told him.

"It's not about that," he said, "you just need to get yourself together."

"But he promised to be with me until the end!" I protested, hot tears rolling down my cheeks. Pulled my tube top up because the draft from my chest area meant a little too much was being exposed, I added, "He wants a divorce."

"Young lady," the pale man said, "you must leave now." He held the center of my back as he walked me out the door.

I indulged my pity party for a few more seconds. The sunlight from the summer sun was beaming down, and the burning smell of a cigarette clung to my nostrils from the woman seated at the front of the building. Maybe she was sleeping with Alex too. A new sense of rejection enveloped me. The same feeling I felt when I learned my mother wasn't ever coming back. That was the day she left my hair damp long enough for me to lather it up on my own. I rinsed the suds out as she directed, and sat at the foot of the bed, waiting for her to braid her magic. A seven-year-old girl's agony was only realized after the six suitcases I helped packed the night before disappeared along with her.

"You'll be okay," the pale man said.

I wondered, *would I?* Standing in the bleak silence, I hoped Alex would change his mind after all. But he didn't. Sliding my cell phone out of my purse, I searched my contact menu for Alex's name, and changed it from "hubby" to "*enemy.*" I followed that with an "I love you" text message to the *enemy.*

Within a few seconds, my phone beeped his reply message: "Go home."

By the time I pulled in front of my driveway, my head was spinning. All I could think of was getting into bed. My tears were all dried out. Pharah's yellow cruiser sat idling in my driveway. Wiping my sadness away, I inspected my face for further signs of disarray. Pharah approached my car with a forced smirk on her face. The same one she always wore when she wanted something.

"Hey," she said. Her ashen black face and twisted jet-black hair fell in locks. "I'm sorry I stopped by unannounced," she said, "but you haven't answered any of my calls."

I was doing a much better job of avoiding her than I thought. "I've been busy," I said, stepping out of the car.

"I've missed you," she said. She hugged my limp body as if she were unsure if that was the appropriate way to hug as sisters. We hadn't touched in so many years, I stopped counting.

"Are you in our sister's wedding or not?" she asked.

Truthfully, I hadn't put much thought into it, other than *no, no* and *no.* Let's see, the advantages of participating in our sister's wedding: it'll make Momma happy. Disadvantages: I'll have to

70

pretend like I care, go there alone, and spend money I don't have while ignoring how my parents tried to make my life a living hell.

I shook my head in disgust.

"What's wrong?" she said.

"I'm going out," I replied, shoving her out of my way as I hurried into my house and slammed the door behind me.

Chapter 15 Pharah

I WOKE UP WITH ANOTHER HEADACHE, but refused to allow it to ruin my plans for the day. With less than a week before Naomi's wedding, getting everyone in the proper gear had become my number one priority. I pulled up in front of the Starbucks drive-through for a cup of coffee.

Dear Lord, when will you find someone for me? I whispered beneath the turtleneck that protected my lips from the chilly air.

"Is that all?" the blonde-haired, female cashier asked. She had a head set in her ears.

"Yes." I said, adding, "God bless you, dear."

Going without a date to Naomi's wedding wasn't as bad as my baby sister getting married before me, but maybe it was even worse when your ex-boyfriend and his wife were invited to the same wedding.

"It's going to happen for you soon, Pharah," Naomi reiterated a few weeks back, as though guilt were lurking somewhere in the room, but she refused to acknowledge it.

I shared the sentiment. She was another one under the age of thirty who was waving single status goodbye. There weren't many singles left, like my best friend, Clara, who dated for six months when her fiancé popped the question in the middle of a highway. Or my cousin, Shelly, who decided after dating her boyfriend, Gregory, for three years that she'd force him to commit by proposing marriage herself. He accepted! So that makes three. All younger, too, but certainly not as deserving as I thought I was.

I know I'm judging, Lord, but I'm only human.

Maybe if I stopped thinking about it, he'd appear somehow for me. But I prevented those thoughts from clouding my mind for very long. For more than five years, I didn't think, speak, or dream of any involvement with the opposite sex. I wished I could snap a finger and just say, "Hey you!" while pointing directly into the face of the enemy. "Yeah you, the single one. The word that's trying to hop into her brain, and stir up trouble; stay the heck out of there!"

It took so much of my energy. I pulled on to Glancier Lane and blew my horn, hinting for Rachel to *get a move on.* The eerie silence in my Toyota Camry was tangible enough to squeeze me

72

right out of the car. The construction workers' loud drilling echoed through my car window, but failed to damper the thoughts in my head.

The less I think about having a boyfriend–or Elsie-the more likely my future love will appear. Less pushiness, and more patience. RECITE AGAIN, but this time, believe it. Less pushiness, and strive to be more patient instead.

I warmed up to the idea of leaving the world behind. *The less often I think about a boyfriend, the more likely he will appear.* RECITE AGAIN. *It will work. Put it out in the air for the universe to welcome it. He will appear. Less pushiness. more patience. RECITE AGAIN. The less I worry about it, the more likely he will appear.*

I looked out of my car window and checked for signs of Rachel. *Where was she?*

Again. *The less I worry about it, the more likely he will appear.*

What is she doing in there? Tapping the steering wheel, it felt like I was playing the numbers game with my sister.

LESS WORRY. HE'LL ARRIVE.

Taking a look over at Rachel's front door, I saw that it wasn't opened. I turned on the radio, and twisted the volume to its peak. *I'm going to give her one more minute.*

RECITE again. The less I worry about it...

And, like a bullet shooting up in the air with no target, I pounded my fist on the horn.

...the more likely he will APPEAR.

CHAPTER 16 Rachel

I HUNG OUT WITH CARSON LAST NIGHT much longer than I anticipated. I'm moving slower than usual. Carson, said he wanted to *"talk"* about how I avoid him even though I didn't think I was doing so purposefully. He doesn't understand how difficult it is finding a sitter for Ashley. Even after I told him she was in the house for an hour, asleep, and I needed to check on her, he insisted I make up for it by giving him a royal head treatment.

I woke up early Thursday morning to get Ashley ready. I was expecting Pharah to be by any minute for our scheduled dress fitting. I had Ashley dressed comfortably since our eleven a.m. appointment could easily turn into a five-hour shopping excursion. Definitely, if Pharah pulled her *she needs to look really good* stuff again for the wedding.

I didn't get much rest last night since Bruce's late night call asking to see Ashley didn't end well. He hadn't seen her in more than four years. I'd done all I could do to reunite them. I even went to visit him in prison, and put her through the horrors of the officers digging in all parts of her body, thinking I was doing what was right for him. My guilty pleasure, satisfying him over me! There're not enough prayers in the world to fix my poor judgments.

I sent him money even though he depleted my bank account, then sold Ashley's television before I finally had the courage to press charges against him.

"I don't know, Bruce," I said while I lay wrapped in my bed covers last night after I'd had enough of his whining. "I'll have to think about whether I can let you see her."

My nerves kept dancing around and making me uneasy. Naturally, he gave me the old-fashioned guilt trip over "all I've done for you!" And I didn't have the guts to tell him he was crazy. Ashley was old enough to recognize faces. His wasn't familiar. I don't get why I should have to force him on her now, since she never abandoned him to begin with.

It didn't matter how many times I tried, there was no satisfying him. No matter how many years, it still didn't change how I felt.

Would he disappoint Ashley as many times as he disappointed me? Wasn't protecting her my only job? Why didn't he get it?

Besides, where did he think he would see her? I certainly couldn't trust him in my house lest he sneak off with my only television and blame it on my *landlord* again! Or would Ashley's screams over being left alone in a studio apartment be heard by my neighbors again while I was at work? Then, I'm sure he'd provide another lame explanation, like the one I fell for, about looking for work. At six-thirty in the morning!

Who would be the next person I begged to bring my daughter home after being questioned by police and social services for allowing an addict so near her? And when cpi;d I stop having to tell Momma the rent money she'd been sending through Ashley's diaper bag had disappeared, along with Bruce's common sense? Too many people had already been let down in too short of time.

I was just afraid of the risk. And he should have known that. Maybe that's why he suggested "your Momma's house" or "you pick the location," as his polite move for tackling me into another trap of downright deception.

I put the last few hair balls on the ends of Ashley's curly, black pigtails as she slept, and kissed her pudgy, *kiss me* cheeks while tickling her with the tip of my nose. I grabbed a few of her favorite toys and tossed them inside my pocketbook.

By the sound of the horn outside, Pharah was waiting on me. I locked the door behind me and ran down the few flights of stairs to meet her.

"About time," Pharah said when I stepped inside her car and was immediately deafened by the sounds of gospel music.

I snapped Ashley in the car seat and she rode with her hands over her ears, her glassy eyes kicking back at me.

"You knew what time we were meeting," she said. "Make plans so they can work out. I just don't understand why that's so hard."

She rolled the knob of the radio, alleviating the throb in my ear. Pharah rolled her eyes before hitting the gas like her patience had worn thin.

"I'm sorry."

It didn't matter what I said, by the way her lips were sagging, I almost felt like I was invading her space. She looked constipated. She was right, after all, I needed to put my plans in motion. I just wished I knew how.

Putting my arm around her shoulder, I said, "Sorry, Pharah, and don't worry, I'll make sure not to do it again."

"It's all right."

I jiggled my head in agreement, and she jiggled her head, saying, "no worries here, he'll appear!"

CHAPTER 17 Pharah

I LOVED EVERYTHING ABOUT wedding dresses, and not just because I wanted to be in one someday. The fluffiness, and fancy, white, clean, untainted freshness almost made me feel reborn again. The ugly in me disappeared when the dress sparkled; it illuminated the entire room. I can only imagine how the day would be when I stood with my handsome prince by my side at the altar and we stared at each other with unmasked desire.

Pink and purple flowers would fill the church and be tightly clenched in my bridesmaids' hands.

My friends, colleagues and church family would naturally all invited for my special event.

The audience would crowd in, eagerly to hear me say the much awaited words, "I do."

The harpist's fingers pluck tunes straight from the heart. My hair would be pulled back under a white veil, and my face airbrushed into a smooth chocolate beauty, so everyone could see.

"I've made it," I'd say. I've reached my dreams, and arrived at my destiny. The one I planned for as many years as I could count.

Now, here I was, combing my fingers through the soft, satin creases, being careful not to disturb the crystals held by a fine thread. Not a single soul in the dress warehouse had a frown. Young, fertile women stood before their mothers, modeling different gowns for their big day. Humbled, yet chosen. I skimmed my hands one final time up and down the train of the dress.

"Why are you putting your hands on it?" the voice grumbled behind me. I spun around only to find Cynthia facing me. I avoided ruining my love affair with the dress by taking it off the lacy hanger, and leading the way to the back of the store, while pretending her verbal attack didn't affect me.

"Well, greetings to you."

"Rachel's somewhere around here with Ashley," I said, anxious to dismiss Cynthia's usual negative energy.

Clutching the bottom of the dress in one hand, and the hanger in the other, I muttered, "I'm going to try on this dress." I wove my way around like I was maneuvering in and out of traffic. Cynthia followed close behind.

"That's the closest you'll ever get to wearing one of those unless *you* start doing something about it," Cynthia snapped.

I raised my eyes to the DRESSING ROOM sign, in hopes of draining Cynthia's voice from my head.

"Rachel!"

I was certain Rachel couldn't hear me, but my loud voice did shut Cynthia up.

Staying focused on the aisles leading to the dressing room, I scanned the rows and rows of nothing but dresses, grazing the back of my free hand past them and only stopping when I was right to the edge of the dressing room door.

"Where's your mom, girlie?" I asked Ashley whose pink barrettes played bungee above her eye. Her lips were stained blue by the lollipop she held while pointing to the dressing room with her hand.

"I'm in here," Rachel said, "trying on a dress."

"I'm going to try on one too."

Cynthia headed for the body-length mirror, flopped the sunglasses off her face and instantly wished she hadn't. A vessel had popped out under her eye, and judging by the black ring, it still hadn't healed.

"How's your eye?" I asked before cupping my hand over my mouth. I was embarrassed by my question, but my inner, wicked voice persisted. "Does it hurt?"

A thin line wrinkled above Cynthia's forehead as a puzzled expression appeared on her face.

"So you're serious about the restraining order thing?" I asked.

She scrunched up her lips, and I cowardly stepped back and waited for her to say something. "Don't ask me about that," she growled.

Creeping my way into the dressing room, I hurried to try on the dress: a size sixteen, strapless beauty with a train as long as a python's tail. Slipping the dress on feet first, I yanked it up to the top of my bust. I tucked the back in with both hands and dragged the zipper until it couldn't zip any further. Fingers aching, and one hand almost numb, by the third try, I took in a deep breath and held my stomach in as I pushed harder. The dress refused to budge along with my determination to get into it. My fingers, now heavy as lead, began to shake. I let out a groan: an urgent sign I should keep my plan in place.

"Rachel!" I called out. Suddenly, it began moving. Up, AND UP it went!

Without warning, Cynthia pushed open the saloon doors that kept public eyes from seeing me. The blackened lens of her eye hung like a worn window blind and she said without hesitation, "Oh, Pharah, that's a mess!"

Chapter 18 Cynthia

MAYBE IT WAS THE WAY James looked at me after I called him a criminal that made me feel bad. His empty expression suggested he was ready to shrink. His facial appearance was blank and sad, causing me to feel obligated to take his telephone number. And his eyes crossed as if I were telling him a big fat lie. In the one year since I'd been practicing law, I never had a client trick me.

That was partly the reason why I couldn't get enough sleep last night. The eyes crossing, their brightness gone. I could probably blame it partly on the vast amounts of weed he'd sucked down his lungs. Or was it the sight of Pharah, torturously squeezing herself into that beautiful wedding dress? Maybe not.

It wasn't like I was criticizing the direction his life had taken. He violated laws for reasons, I never assumed were valid. I was making a logical hypothesis based on past and present clients who also didn't follow rules. *LIKE ANDRE!*

I could easily break laws too. I'd sure like to run a few red lights when I'm late for an appointment, or double park in a fire lane for a quick trip to the mall, but I don't because the punishment isn't worth it. That was all I meant. That was it. He has more guts than I do, and obviously, doesn't mind the punishment. Since he's so proud to accept it, he should easily have understand where I stood in the matter. *But no.* He decided to take a portion of what I said and blow it into something serious. And then, he gave me a half-hearted hug before walking away. It was one of those *let me get this raggedy chick away from me so I can be on my way* hugs. Like I was getting on his nerves. I shouldn't have stopped for him. If only I'd known. I'll fix him good. I'll be seeing him around. I'll make certain of that.

Stepping inside my parents' home, I looked behind the door after I entered. The volume of the television in the family room was in full blast; no wonder Momma was always yelling.

"Momma!"

Pastor was sitting in one corner of the room where the television watched him. His eyes were glued to his newspaper. "She's in the kitchen," he said.

I thought for a very brief moment of inviting him to avoid repeating my announcement, but then decided against it. As soon as he heard Andre's name mentioned, he'd tune me out. As he did with everything that was unrelated to his congregants.

"Hey Pops," I said. He nodded as he usually did when he didn't want to be bothered. After I peeked at myself in the wall mirror, I went into the kitchen, and took a seat in the middle of Momma's round dinner table. She stood at the sink, washing the dishes by hand. That was something I hadn't been accustomed to lately. Humming her usual church melodies, I slipped the restraining order out and placed it on top of the table, nervous to share my secret.

Maybe it was the mean glare I was guaranteed to see once she made it known she wasn't satisfied with my answer, but whatever facade she chose to wear today, I was ready for the fight. I took a deep breath and pretended the court order I stacked on my left was a paying client and Momma was the judge.

"Keep him away from me," I said to her.

Momma swung around from the sink like I'd taken her by surprise. The mean look quickly appeared. Slipping my dark shades off my face, I hoped to get a small ounce of sympathy.

"I don't want to argue, Momma," I said. "I got an order for him to stay away." Dangling the protective order in front of me as if it were a fish out of water, I explained, "I can't let him beat on me like that! You know it isn't right."

The wrinkles on Momma's face didn't move, not a centimeter. She stood with her hands on both hips as if unsure what to make of it. My hands were tired now from all the movement so I dropped it back on the table and waited for *Meany* to begin her spiel.

That's your brother! What will the church say? How's he supposed to go to Naomi's wedding?

And my answers would follow: *He'll still be my brother, the church can't heal my eye, and he doesn't believe in the sanctity of marriage anyway.*

Momma took her wet hands and slapped them on the sides of her apron. Opening the cabinet above her head, she peeled out a manila envelope, and glided a sheet of paper out before slamming it next to my "client."

Then she turned her back to me and went on with washing her dishes.

I pretended I couldn't see the bold letters addressed to Andre that read: *VIOLATION OF PROBATION HEARING.* I thought about apologizing for causing such a stir, but before I could, she started in again with her humming.

Chapter 19 Naomi

I HAD BEEN IN THE BABY store for about an hour when I decided to skip the bridal store with my sisters and spend the last two hours of Norman's shift at Babies R Us in search of baby bargains. I thought it was better to shop for Jessa than for me, even though my wedding loomed in less than five days. Baby accessories had more value than the phony elegance that my wedding represented. The wedding took a big hit on my budget, which Norman didn't hesitate reminding me frequently about. I was spending my own money for my dress and accessories; and of course, without a job, that translated into the need to solicit Norman. Norman hated spending money, unless it was spent on him.

I wanted a white, wooden crib for Jessa that matched the pink teddy bears I'd been collecting for her. I went to two different Babies R Us, hoping to find a real Naomi-type of bargain, which didn't require me to ask the family for donations. But, of course, the only ones that fitted into NAOMI'S BARGAINS were out of stock.

"How much is this one?" I asked the saleswoman who took longer to help me than I would have liked.

The crib set floor model was featured in the middle of the store, and appeared to be the most suitable for Jessa.

"Let me check for you," the saleswoman replied.

I brought a two-page list of "must haves" that I'd written the night before. However, our budget could only cover one of the thirteen items listed. I was afraid Norman would cross out more than half of my list once he realized we were the ones paying the bill.

"It's two hundred, thirty-seven dollars," the saleswoman said. Her curly blonde hair was tossed in a spongy. She beamed a smile as I walked around the crib, envisioning Jessa kicking her small toes in it while I kept snapping photos of her.

"Are we ready to check out?" the saleswoman inquired.

"Well, I'm still looking for now. I'm sorry."

"It's okay. Just let me know if you need more help."

Two hundred, thirty-seven dollars for Christ's sake?

She pulled the spongy ponytail holder from her head and flung the long strands of hair down her back.

Dropped myself on the rocking chair, I kicked my feet on the footrest while waiting for Norman to get off work. He'd already pulled in over fifty-two hours this week with plans to work more. He blamed his overtime hours on our imminent baby arrival since Momma told him to do it. But I guessed there had to be a 2014 video game release scheduled some time in the next few weeks, although he wasn't divulging any information.

I crushed the list into my pocket and prayed it would magically reappear in the shape of a crib, and be delivered into Jessa's bedroom, inside a house we could afford. Closing my eyes, I dozed and daydreamed about Norman holding Jessa's hand and mine while taking a long walk in Fairmont Park without ever stopping for his mandated cigarette break. Without his worries and complaints about my cooking, my weight, and my snoring.

"I'm tired as heck!" The roar of Norman's voice reverberated in my head. He stood in front of the footrest, holding a treat from McDonald's. I reached for the bag and he hid it behind him.

"Why are you sitting here all out in the open?" he asked. "You don't want to scare these people."

He chuckled. I froze, suddenly afraid my eyes would land on strange bystanders. His caramel brown skin didn't do a good job of hiding his freckles. Norman's body overshadowed everything around him: big, loud and powerful.

"I'm tired too," I replied.

"You haven't worked all day," he reminded me. His ensuing laughter drowned out the words in my head that were bunched together in a knot.

"I know," I said, giving in by way of a smile. I was unwilling to disagree that an extra fifty pounds on a five-foot-two-inch woman was not only an inconvenience, but real work.

I held out my hand as a truce to avoid a mental fight I had grown to expect.

"I can't lift you," he said.

"Come on, babes; help me pull out the chair. My back hurts."

He opened his dark, greasy hands and reached for mine.

"Give me your hands," he said. I hung my hand in the air for a few seconds before I took his.

"Got to work, feed you and pick you up. Give me a break," he said, "help me out, sweet chunky."

Sweet chunky, the nickname I hated.

Let see, as if the mechanic's shirt he was wearing wasn't ironed crisp this morning by my very hand. My swollen fingers used an iron, spewing hot steam on my skin. As if the size eleven sneakers on his feet weren't bought because I stood in line at the Foot Locker for six hours after he insisted on getting a pair of *Michael Jordan's Special Edition,* that went on sale the very same day as my baby's ultrasound appointment!

"The crib's two hundred dollars, babes," I said, breaking the monotony. I had to somehow find a way to work around getting the difference.

He wiped his forehead.

"Two hundred? What it's made of? Gold?" He slapped the crib on its rim, and pushed it until it was no longer centered in the room. "See?" he said. "It's not even durable. I don't want that one."

"I think it'll go nicely with the baby's room. It's cute; don't you think?" I said, standing as close to him as I could without annoying him, but still rooting for Jessa's crib.

"Well, we can find it a little cheaper somewhere else, can't we? At another store?"

I stood motionless in front of the crib, and rubbed my hands over the rails, taking another imaginary peek at Jessa's legs kicking in the crib.

"Uh, I guess," I said.

"Can't you get all this stuff from your baby shower? When are they having one for you anyway?" Norman ripped open the bag of McDonald's and began feasting on the sandwich.

I played with the notion of sending Norman a letter to remind him of the Crieur family rules, which specifically forbade baby showers for unmarried/unwedded hussies like me who thought getting knocked up before jumping the broom was a good idea.

"Hello?" he said. "When are they having one?"

"I don't know, sweetie."

"You're trying to buy all this stuff while your parents keep getting all this money from the church," he said. "Ask them to put some of that money towards this baby."

After he gorged on the sandwich, he added, "I should call your momma 'cause your baby stuff costs too much."

"Yeah," I agreed, "way too much."

85

"Let's get out of here and go home so I can get some rest."

"Yes," I eagerly concurred. "We should do just that; this is way too much. *Way too much.*"

Chapter 20 Bethanny

SHARON AND I SAT AT THE BAR and waited for our drinks. We weren't at Michael's Bar Ring for more than ten minutes before the hungry men began to buzz around us. Tall, short, fat, skinny and a few that I could tell wouldn't know what to do with me. I hadn't been out for a very long time. Sharon spent the last few nights at my house helping with the children.

Alex didn't come home, but his clothes were missing. I'm certain he used his key to drop by while I was out in order to avoid me altogether. However, that didn't stop my calls to his cell phone. He left me in the house with our kids, the house we bought two years ago. The four-bedroom, brick single was my dream home, *our* dream home. Situated in a working class neighborhood, the house boasted a trimmed tree line and white fences. Neighbors were friendly and the area was safe, neat, and quiet.

My children freely played outside without any fear. Security teemed in our home despite its absence in my marriage. I hadn't spoken to any family members since the incident, but felt sure many knew what was happening.

Cynthia dropped by a few hours after Pharah to bleach Alex's belongings. Pharah prayed around the house just before scooping up all three kids for a slumber party. She promised to drop them off at Alex's mother's house in the morning.

It didn't take much to convince Sharon we should hit the streets. I drove my silver mommy minivan and stopped in Lucky's, Brown Sugs, and our final stop, Michael's, for a much-needed, fun night out.

I hadn't partied since the kids were born and the stress of Alex's affair led me back to this part of town. By the time it was eleven at night, I moved about to the music in my chair, recapturing my twenties. By midnight, the bar was packed with sweaty men and women. I rocked back and forth to the *music makes them bounce* stripper music.

Convinced she would get laid tonight, Sharon ran to the ladies' room to freshen up while I sat back on the bar stool, grinding to the music. I swirled up and down on the chair. Twirl, roll, swirl, roll. I pushed my butt harder on the cushion with my eyes closed and rocked from side-to-side as I envisioned Alex's arms wrapped around me.

"Can I buy you a drink?" a gentle male voice whispered in my ear. I halted my moves. The heavy set, tall, middle-aged male pulled the stool out beside me.

"If that's what you want to do," I replied.

He was wearing a green, collared, polyester shirt, white necktie, and satin, shiny, black pants. Slightly overdressed for the club my eyes wandered about, and I felt his grayish eyes staring at me, but I counted to eleven before retreating.

"Laurent," he said, "and your name?" He extended his hand out.

"Bethanny," I replied as I shook his hand, then quickly let go.

Turning to the bartender, he said, "Let her have another of whatever she's drinking and I'll get a peach Zinfandel on the rocks." He spoke with a New York accent.

"You come here often?"

"Not really," I said.

"Didn't think so; you don't look like the type to hang around here," he said. His grin looked as safe as Alexus's once was.

"What does my type look like?"

"I don't know. You don't strike me as the crowd type of woman."

"Oh, whatever," I mumbled.

"So you're here by yourself, hon?"

"No, I'm here with my girlfriend. She's around…" I said, my eyes circling the room for Sharon.

"Your girl?"

"Yeah, my girlfriend, my friend that's a girl." I rolled my eyes.

"Just making sure *us straight*," he stopped to laugh. "Don't want to cross any boundaries, if you know what I mean."

"No boundaries crossed," I said. "Hell I've had my share of fun. No worries."

I took a swig of the drink the bartender delivered in front of me.

"Oh, okay," the man stopped to look at me, then pulled out his wallet to pay. "Fun, huh? So… are you single?"

I couldn't remember the last time I was asked that question since almost everyone I hung around already knew the answer.

"I am now, I guess."

"You guess?" he said. "You're kind of fine there to be a single lady."

"Well, I'm not single. I'm married," I said, suddenly reluctant to release the title.

"Well, all right."

I sipped my third Ciroc, trying to loosen up. I knew it was going to be a long, depressing night: no kids, no husband, and I needed more alcohol to numb me.

"Where's your girlfriend?" he asked.

"Around."

"Got any kids?" he said as I faced him.

"Yup!" I said.

"How many?"

"Four," I sucked the straw tightly around my lips.

"Whoa," he said, "God bless ya, girl."

"Yeah, really." I laughed.

I scanned the bar again for Sharon, but couldn't find her.

"Want another round?" he offered.

"No. I'm good for now; don't you try making me crawl out of here!" I laughed and he joined me. We sat shoulder-to-shoulder and the music bumped in the same rhythm as my heartbeat.

"Do you have boys or girls?"

"Girls, and a boy," I said like I just unleashed an atomic bomb that was ready to do major damage. "I'm married to their father, but he cheated on me."

"Oh, okay." Laurent's left eyebrow pushed up a half inch. "So you're back in the swing of things?"

There lay an uninvited smirk. A telling expression of a possible opportunity.

"Actually, I'm not."

"He's not a smart guy, I take it."

"Why do you say that?"

"Well, look at you!" he said. "If he didn't know how lucky he was, he's not a smart dude."

"Where are you from?"

"Brooklyn, New York, but I'm here on business."

I took a moment to retrace his facial muscles, and hairline. *On business*. That's what Alexus must've said when he cheated on me.

"I can tell."

"Really?"

"I used to stomp around Brooklyn during my younger days, and had some really fun times there. I know New Yorkers."

"Oh, really?" he said.

"Yeah, my girlfriends and I would pretty much come down on weekends for some fun, as well as business," I answered.

The business of night light life: arriving in New York by ten at night and finishing up with your John by three.

"What kind of business?"

"Grownup folk business!" I answered. "What kind of business are you in?"

"I handle banquets and special events for my company. We are trying to expand," he said. "What about you?"

"I raise kids. That's my business."

"Do you want another drink?" he asked. "You're throwing those down, aren't you?"

"I need the buzz right about now," I said. "I'll take another."

"Another Ciroc!" he yelled to the bartender.

"What did you say your name was?"

"Laurent, sweetheart," he answered.

"Laurent, you don't know me and I appreciate what you said earlier. I gave that man my whole life. I gave him my entire life! He hurt me to the core. I gave him three healthy kids," I said after clearing my throat to say more. "I left school, and cooked and cleaned for the bastard who was sleeping around on me! I thought he was working hard to support our family."

"So how many kids do you have? Three or four?"

I sipped my drink "Three: two daughters and a son. Y'all men know how to break a good woman's heart," I said to explain my misfortune. "I'm not going to let that hold me back though."

"Y'all men? No. No," he said, "*he* broke your heart, he and only he. I can't speak for anyone, but myself. I know a lot of women like you who hand over their minds, bodies and souls to those cats who could care less about you."

"He's my husband," I said, protesting his observation. I wasn't like other women. I wasn't the same person. "He won't even tell me what I've done to deserve it."

"Would it matter?"

"Of course, it would!"

"Okay," he said, "I'm just wondering, that's all."

"I've called him almost every night, you know. I suggested that we go to counseling. I've even told him I would wait for him until he was ready, even if it meant him staying with that woman for a few months! All I need is for him to say he'll come home again."

"Did he take you up on your offer?"

I tipped my chin to my chest and replied, "He hasn't responded."

"My advice to you is ignore him. Just work on you. Ignore him for the next few weeks, he's probably waiting for you to call him anyway," he said. "Men loves a desperate weight. Easier for us."

"I ain't desperate," I said, "I just want my family back."

"I know; do what you need to do to get what you want."

"I'm not worrying about him tonight. I'm here to have fun, and here he is, ruining my night. He can kick rocks and die! I don't want anything to do with him right now and neither do my kids."

"How old are your kids?"

"Two, three and five," I said "and now he's trying to take my kids away from me, but he doesn't bother to even visit them."

"I don't think they told you they didn't want their dad around them," he laughed.

"Well, their dad didn't want their mom, so clearly, he didn't want them either."

"You're being unfair, sis," he laughed. "That's not right, sexy; you can't take a man from his kids."

"Really?" I challenged him. "Well, how come my momma didn't get that memo?"

Laurent paused as if he were waiting for another bomb to drop. So I took another sip of my drink.

"I have an eighteen-year-old son, and his mother and I had lots of problems when we broke up sixteen years ago," he said. "Jason was about your son's age, but I hung onto her, sweating her for months and months until she would let me see him. By the time he turned five, he primarily lived with me."

91

He shrugged and continued. "I say that because if he loves his kids, he'll be hounding you until you crack. I'm not telling you what to do, but you should not put a wedge between him and children. Even though Jason's mom and I didn't work out, we agreed we both loved him, so it wasn't fair to separate him from one or the other. It took her a while to understand it, but it eventually worked. Give him some time, and if he truly loves his kids, he will come back for them. If he loves his family, he'll come back for you. If he cares enough, he'll come and get you."

I sniffed and wiped the tear that dripped on the top of my upper lip.

"I'm sorry," he said "didn't mean to get you upset."

"No," I replied. "I just hope you're right. I hope I won't have to wait until hell turns over and he's dead and gone before he decides it's time for him to run back." I laughed until my stomach ached.

The music in the background grew fuzzy in my ears, but I moved my arms and back rhythmically in the chair.

"It's that time, guys," the bartender said.

The bartender delivered my last drink of the night. I was glad Sharon and I decided to come. Although I had no sight of Sharon since she went to the restroom, I hadn't gone looking for her either.

"Do you need a ride home?" Laurent asked in a meek tone.

"No, I drove in with my girlfriend," I said, looking around the bar while the crowd dispersed outside, "but I have no idea where she went."

"I'm not sure you are safe to drive, or go alone. Let me drive you."

If Sharon didn't pop in soon, I'd have to take him up on his offer. My kids weren't home, so even If Laurent turned out to be a murderer, at least, he wouldn't be able to hurt my kids.

"All right, but let me swing around to see if I can spot my car in the lot."

I walked to the corner of the bar and scanned the lot from the window. My car was gone from where I parked. *Sharon must've found herself a date.*

"Where do you live?" he asked, and the warmth from his breath moved the hairs on my neck.

"Over on Providence Street, it's about a half hour away."

"I'll take you," he said.

Chapter 21 Bethanny

I FOLLOWED LAURENT OUT TO the car and felt my blood pressure rising, along with the sun. He stood about six feet tall, and was much heavier than what I was used to. Two black moles stuck out on the right side of his neck, not nearly attractive. I could see him staring from the corners of his eyes.

I walked ahead of him so he could get a better look.

"Right here" he said. He stopped in front of an old, four-door Range Rover.

"Cool," I said.

He put the keys in the passenger side door to let me in. Once inside, I reached over to unlock the driver's side door, as I'd seen in the *Bronx Tale* movie, but of course, the door was already unlocked. My body loosened up in the cool breeze that lingered in the air between us. I felt unbound, and free. I shouted out my address with wild abandon.

The car ride was quiet and I grew curious to know more about Mr. Laurent. He was not as bad looking as I first thought. And didn't smell bad. My house was empty. By the time his car stopped in front of my door, my mind was already made up.

"Want to come in?"

The crooked smirk on his face didn't have me completely convinced he was wary of my proposition.

"For?" he replied.

I shot out a glare, like the kind I'd have given Alex when he tried to avoid a pointed question.

"Are you sure? There's no masked man in there trying to get me? "he asked. "Is your husband going to like the idea of having me in his house?"

"If he cared, he would be here," I mumbled. "Come on in."

I got out of the car, and rummaged through my purse for my house keys. I hoped Alex hadn't decided to move back in while I was out. I would have to explain where I picked up Laurent and why he was here at this hour.

Mr. Charlie, my nosy neighbor, turned on his kitchen lights, so I jammed my key into the door and ushered Laurent in.

"Are you hungry?" I asked, kicking Max's toy Spiderman trucks to one side of the room before switching on my light.

"No, I'm fine."

"Are you sure? I can make a mean dish."

"No, I'm good," he said, rubbing his hand over his stomach. "Got any good music?" he asked.

"Um… let me see." I went up to my bedroom and shut the door behind me. I held my back to the door, and closed my eyes to eradicate the immediate sense of anger that began to rise inside me. Skimming through what was left of Alex's CDs, I shuffled through the Bethanny J, Keisha Cole, and Tupac, the final choices for tonight. Plugging in the CD player, I popped the CD in and let Bethanny J tell my side of the story.

Had he considered how I would feel?

Had he considered our children?

I stood in the middle of the room as the music played and imagined dancing on stage with Alex as the only audience member. Wiggling my shoulders, I dropped down on my ankles while Laurent sat on my sofa with a big smile on his face. His shoes were removed, and his tie was loosened. I moved my hips like a cake mixer, and swirled my body around to the music while letting my eyes flirt with Laurent.

I swerved from side-to-side before backing my behind right in front of him. I took my time to unbutton my top, waving my arms to allow my shirt to slide from underneath me.

I rubbed my hands on the sides of my breasts, and moved up and down, letting my nipples stand out like an exhibit. Dropping low to the floor, I spread my legs wide and let my bottom face him. Flexing my legs wider to look at him from between them, I tossed my bra to the sofa where he sat. Jiggling my breasts, I moved my waist on the floor as if I were riding Alex.

Push. Hard. Swirl to the melody. Kiss my nipples. Remove my underwear. Let it all hang out. Laurent was seated comfortably on the recliner and grinned. He grinned wide and his face turned red, a recognizable expression from my past. The *I dare you to stare* and *you know you want it* mind-read was revealed by his thick arched eyebrow. Not sure I wanted to, but I went with it. He ran to me like a quarterback reaching for the football and smacked my butt. I could feel the skin of my butt stinging so I stepped away to rub my hands up and down my naked body.

Moving in on him slowly, I kissed his lips and neck before pushing him with me on top of him onto the sofa. Raising my right leg over his left shoulder, I climbed my way over onto his face. I let him help himself to some of me until he muscled my leg away and pulled me into his mouth. I twisted. And moaned. And held Laurent's head against me as I felt him moving inside. I squeezed my thighs against his face and kept my body steady while my legs shook.

"Yes," I said, biting into the edge of the sofa. Then, in a whisper, "Alex."

He lifted me up by my legs and moved me to the living room floor. He began pushing himself deeply inside me, so deeply, I had to hold my breath. Five, four, three, two, *yes.*

I closed my eyes so I wouldn't see any sign of excitement from him. Drilling a cardboard image of Alex over the stranger's head, Laurent's moaning was a distraction. I gripped Laurent tighter to bring him closer, and his body jerked in my arms before he played dead. The moisture in the air was filled with the stench of two wet, naked bodies.

"That was good, baby," he said, "that was real good."

His comment launched me into a silent rage. I buried my nose deeply into my armpit. Maybe the scent from my own body could bring me back to planet Earth.

Chapter 22 Andre

SPRAWLED ACROSS THE QUEEN-SIZED bed, I checked my cell phone for messages. I got up early because I thought I heard a knock in the middle of the night on our bedroom door. I was initially afraid the judge had ordered me back to jail after learning about Cynthia's punch, but it turned out the door bandit was my daughter, Ella, who squeezed her little body in between her mother and me.

I ignored the urges for a hit, since I feared I'd wake Monique. The last thing I needed was to give her another reason to get my blood boiling. "You're smoking again," or "I'm leaving you" she would no doubt say.

Her monthly promises were running on empty. I already had enough on my plate, which was just the reason why I needed white to calm me.

I heard Monique grooving in the kitchen to Luther Vandross's "Here and Now." She was trying to put together something to eat, finally. When she did cook, it was always missing some ingredient or another. Pancakes, but no syrup. Eggs, but no ketchup. Bacon without eggs, and cereal without bananas. Her meals were never complete.

The aroma from the pork bacon forced me out of bed. I sat up against the headboard, thinking about how to get a few dollars from Shirley. With only thirty-three cents left in my pocket, I did not have enough to get more white. Monique's feet thumped up the stairs as she stepped into the bedroom with an unsealed white envelope in her hand.

"Andre,'" Monique said as she stepped inside the bedroom with a grin on her face, "Look at this!"

She tossed what was a sealed, certified envelope onto the bed. *Whatever it was had better impress me*, I thought. I read the return address of the envelope, COURT OF COMMON PLEAS. Yawning, I opened it.

"Well? What is it?"

"I haven't had a court date in six months and I haven't committed any major crimes to warrant a revisit." I gulped. "What they want from me?" I asked.

"What does it say?" Monique asked, hovering over my shoulder, "just read what it says."

No news is typically good news, but by the look of things, nothing good was coming out this one. CYNTHIA CRIEUR VS. ANDRE CRIEUR was as much as I needed to see. I HATED THAT GIRL, CYNTHIA. She wouldn't help me get a job, or put food on my table, or offer anything towards my court fees; and all she could think to do was make life for me and my family even more miserable.

Biting the bottom of my lip and tasting the salty blood in mouth, I thought, *if my probation officer gets wind of this, nothing good will come of it.* I paced back and forth, gnawing at the inside of my cheeks and trying to think of ways to fix it, like going to her job and sending flowers, or calling Momma and asking her to talk to her.

"Where are you going?" Monique asked.

"I have to go back to court," I say, "or they bringing me back in."

"Now?"

"No." I tossed the mail on the side of the floor and replied, "She's trying to send me to jail."

Monique grew wide-eyed as she gripped the sides of her tummy. I never gave her my version of my sneak attack on Cynthia. Now that she'd taken it this far, I kind of wished I'd kicked her.

"Who?"

"Cynthia," I said.

"Everything is good; I can feel it," Monique said as if to flick the reality of what I said away. Her dreamy eyes became as clouded as the weather. I crossed my eyes in disgust, wrinkled my lips, and pretended she wasn't there.

"Everything is going to work out. No need to worry," she said, careful so her tone wouldn't ignite the fire smoldering inside me. The fire that raged from the fuel caused by the world being so unpleasant to me. Always struggling to be understood, and respected, and be seen as the man that I was, yet but still, my flaws were always placed in the forefront.

"You know, I'm just trying to fly straight," I said. "I have my kid, my wife, and my new baby coming. What else can a man want?"

"We going to be good" she said, wiping the corner of her chin. "Everything's going to work out."

It had better. I rubbed the spine of her back. "Just keep me better fed so I can be strong enough to find a job," I said.

Not that I was looking, since most places I applied wanted a clean record. And I couldn't guarantee clean piss neither.

I got up from the bed and stood at the window. The gray clouds moved along the sky as if it were shaping for a storm. My signals said today wouldn't be a good day. My remedy? Scooter. My mind wasn't at ease, so I'd have to figure out a way to sweet talk Shirley into getting me some more white.

"Yes," she said, "a job!" Monique jumped on my back and wrapped her legs around my waist. I used my arms to hold her. "We should call the lawyer," she said. I drilled my eyes into Monique, chewing on my bottom lip for a quick response. "Talk to him to see if any of this affects your criminal case," she added.

Henry Davenport was my lawyer. I hadn't paid him in more than six months. And even though Monique thought she was paying him, that didn't stop him from sending me invoices, which I forwarded to Momma.

"He don't know anything," I said, figuring my insult would shut her bad idea up.

"Of course, he does," she said, unconvinced. "I'm going to call him."

Monique's legs dropped to the floor, and she stood at the foot of the bed with her cell phone in hand as I clenched my fingers around hers. Then I slid my hand into hers to ease the phone out of it. I shook my head as quickly as my heart raced. "I don't know," I said, "but I'll take care of it tomorrow."

"We should call him now, sweetie,"

"I haven't paid him yet."

The wariness in Monique's expression suggested she wasn't buying it. "How's that?" she said. "I gave you the money,"

And I spent it, Monique. On the night you kicked me out, after making a call to my friend, Leroy, who said I wasn't there. You threw every shoe I owned out of the closet. Instead of enduring a one round boxing match with her, I left. I took all of Henry's four hundred and seventy dollars and smoked it. Me and Shirley. *We* smoked.

"Haven't had time to pay him," I said, "but I'm going to take care of it soon. You know, with Naomi's wedding and trying to find work, I haven't had any time to go down to his office."

I began looking for my pants and hoped she wouldn't check to see if there were any remnants of cash in them.

Then I worked my way back to Monique and grabbed her by the waist and kissed her lips. Be assertive. Forthcoming. Authoritative, and she couldn't resist.

"Let me worry about those things," I said.

Monique hesitated to say another word and I knew she didn't believe me. I'd never given her any reason to. She'd caught my hand inside her purse too many times to count. And she found Shirley's, as well as other friends' undergarments in man-made hiding places that she wasn't supposed to find. I did what I could to make her believe in me, but I couldn't do much about it since I didn't have faith in myself.

Her passion for me was incredible, however, and she more often than not took me at my word even when she shouldn't have. She let out a half-hearted sigh, "Well, okay, Andre." Then she added, "I love you, baby."

"Love you, too," I shot back. I covered her back with my hand as she tucked her head under my chin.

"I can't wait until you walk me in that church with all those women who wants what I have," she said. Monique's skin glowed like a firefly. "I can't wait for this wedding day!" she said.

She yanked her head back, examining me like a newborn baby. The thought of Shirley being seated in the audience of the church while Monique and I did as Monique planned was making me nervous.

"I may not be able to walk you in," I said, "but I'll be right there."

Monique rolled her eyes as if my response wasn't part of the game plan. "Whatever," she said. "As long as we're near each other," she added as she squeezed her arms around my waist. "They'll get the picture, all of them."

I cupped my hand over my eyes to mentally wipe away Shirley's face once she realized my wife and I weren't really sleeping in two separate bedrooms after all.

"Where's my breakfast? I'm hungry."

"It's almost done," she said, "let me show you something." Monique opened the bedroom closet, and rummaged through it.

"What are you looking for?"

"Let me show you the dress I'm wearing," she said. Jumping up and down like she was swinging from a bungee pad, she clapped her hands in excitement as she reached into the closet and pulled out a red, spaghetti-strap dress, which she hugged before putting it around her waist. The bottle-shaped, lace dress fell to her ankles. Its V-shaped neck was carved into the bust. She pulled off her shirt and slipped on the dress. Standing in front of the mirror nailed to the bedroom closet, she twirled.

"Whoa!" I said, "where are you going dressed like that and with that belly?"

"To Naomi's wedding," she said, "you like?"

If only she had a little more flesh in her thighs, and a little more meat in her legs, her dress would have looked more appealing. The pregnancy bump didn't help either. I smacked my right hand on Monique's behind. "You look great, baby," I said.

She spun around and dropped a heavy kiss on my cheek. I rubbed my belly to dampen the groaning sounds of my hunger. "I'm hungry," I repeated.

Monique's cooking wasn't anything to write home about. I wished she could have put her pride on the burner, instead of what she called a "meal," and asked Momma for some help with her cooking.

"I know, sweetie," she said. "I'm making a big one today."

"And put ketchup on my hash browns too."

"I didn't make any hash browns," she said, "just bacon and eggs."

"Salt and pepper," I said as I followed her out and made my way into the bathroom.

"No salt, just pepper."

I stretched in the middle of the room and pushed my big toe deeply into the plush carpeting, just enough for a rug burn. GOOD GRIEF!

She hummed to Chaka Khan's "Every Woman" as she hurried down the stairs. I looked over my shoulder, making sure she was out of sight, and flushed the toilet to sound busy as I tiptoed out of the bathroom. Shutting the door softly behind me, I reached in the closet, and got the good book out before the shoeboxes above my head came tumbling down. I scrambled to put them away.

Quickly opening the Bible, I dug my hand inside to sift through the white and pour what was left of the contents on Ella's drawing paper instead of foil. I lit the lighter, and waited for the white to morph into liquid. Then I closed my eyes with the pipe in hand and opened my lips to let the gray cloud escape.

Marriage sucks, Monique's cooking sucks, and I don't care what Shirley has to do, but she'll have to get me another hit.

"Daddy!" Ella's vibrant voice sprang into the bedroom, and I slid the pipe beneath the mattress as I quickly removed myself from the bed.

"What are you doing, Daddy?" her little voice squeaked.

Her emerald-green eyes were plagued with curiosity. I fanned the room with my hands before cracking open the window, and held the twenty-eight-pound giant in my arms.

"Why aren't you asleep, baby?" I asked.

As clever as her tender age of four could be, she replied, "It's morning, Daddy. I'm not sleepy."

Her tresses hung down to her shoulders. She pouted her lips as she always did to get her way. I kept her as close to the door as possible.

"I told you to knock, honey," I said. "Remember?" She dropped her head on my shoulder and nodded into my shoulder blades. "Okay, baby, well, Daddy will be right out," I said as I let her out into the hall. "I'll be right back."

Monique's slippers swooshed on the stairs and I hurried back into the bedroom to grab the pipe and throw it under the bed.

"Are you hungry, Ella?" Monique asked her, and she crossed her arms in a hissy fit. "Why are you standing there, baby? Go ahead in," Monique said. Ella looked back at me, and I looked away.

"Daddy says to wait," Ella said.

"Where do you want this?" Monique asked. She was referring to her morning creation.

"Just put it down on the dresser," I told her, now irritated by all the distractions.

"What's wrong with you?" she asked as I pushed the closet door closed.

"Nothing."

Monique walked around to the other side of the bed as if putting me on notice. She placed the plate and cup on the dresser, and studied me closely. "Why are your eyes so glassy?" she asked.

I blinked a few times to erase her suspicions.

"What are you talking about?" I replied.

Monique. Mrs. Know-it-all. I took the tastefully arranged colored plate of bacon and pancakes and laid it on my lap. Then I swallowed without chewing, like my life depended on it.

"There you go, tripping again."

"Is it okay to come in now, Daddy?" Ella asked. She stood close to my leg, so I plugged a few bites into her mouth to keep her from talking.

"Yes, it's cool."

I kissed her tiny face while Monique kept her eyes fastened on me.

"You were smoking, weren't you?" Monique said.

"Come on now, Monique. I'm trying to eat and you on some nonsense right now!"

Monique pulled the closet door open, and I jumped. I laid the plate on the bed, but not fast enough for Monique. She squirmed her hands in between the mattress and the floor and raised my pipe in her hand, like she was wielding a sword.

"Give it to me," I said.

I took the pipe out of her hand and shoved it into my pocket. Monique became motionless, and didn't resist. I could feel the heat from her body permeating the room. Her eyes were as red as peppers and her teeth were gnashing.

"You got to go," she said. "You need to get out of here! I told you about bringing that stuff in this house."

Cuffing my hand over her mouth, I shook her like a rag doll. Her words, and the impending criticism, no doubt, troubled me. "I'm not going anywhere," I said. "Calm down!"

Ella covered her ears with her tiny hands. "Leave my mommy alone, Daddy," she said.

"Back up!" I yelled to Ella who clung to her mother's legs as she cried. She reached her arms toward Monique so she could pick her up. "Nobody told you to be so nosy," I reprimanded Monique.

I threw on a hoodie and jeans and walked away from another argument, caused by her, as if my other problems weren't enough.

"You're not ever going to change," she said, "you're not even trying."

I charged out the room and she followed me. Her river of tears drowned out her face as she held the subpoena up and waved it around like a flag.

"You're not serious about us!" she shouted at the top of her lungs.

"You acting stupid right now," I told her.

Ella began to cry again, burying her little face under her mother's swollen belly.

"You're the one stressing me, man," I said. "I told you I was going to stop, but you keep nit-picking."

Monique dropped her head in her hand. "I'm sorry, Andre," I put my arms around her shoulders while hoping to bring our disagreement to a calm harbor before making my exit.

"I don't want to get my girls upset," I said, "but you've got to stop this."

Monique clung to my waist and wouldn't let me go.

"Don't leave," she begged.

Her lips quivered when she spoke, but I looked beyond the fear and desperation in her face, and stepped over her body to get away.

"I don't want you to leave," she pleaded again.

She never let me go without a fight. But I had no energy left for it.

I gathered my Bible and made sure everything was still intact, before reaching under the bed for my pipe. Throwing my sweater over my back, I kissed my two tearful angels on my way out.

"I will see you in a few days," I said. "I got to clear my head."

Monique held her lips together, but struggled to keep them closed. "Where are you going?" she asked.

"Momma's," I fibbed.

Monique remained silent, like a trapped lion, looking for an escape, while Ella jammed her thumb in her mouth and bounced on her hips. Monique's doleful face didn't help, but it didn't stop me either. I left.

"I'm sorry," she said, "if you leave now, don't bother coming back."

"Oh, come on, Monique. I'll be back in a few days. I hate it when you're pregnant," I said. "You're too sensitive and annoying."

Hurrying down the steps, I opened the front door to a man who was dressed in all black. A bicycle helmet was attached to his head. Baby-blue eyes keyed into mine. His messenger bag was attached to his shoulders.

"Is there an Andre Crieur here?" he asked.

I hesitated for a moment, wondering if the day had finally arrived for me. My probation was either revoked, or there was someone out to get me. I'd have to go back to jail and face that stinky hole again. Maybe I could run! I estimated about twenty inches between us. His skinny arms couldn't catch me. Maybe being polite and straightforward could get me out of this one. I erased the frown clinging to my face and stretched my lips into a convincing smile.

"Who's asking?"

"Are you Mr. Crieur?" he said.

I bobbed my head in affirmation.

"You've been served," the man said before shoving the manila envelope in my hand and hopping on his bicycle to speed away.

Chapter 23 Rachel

I DELETED THE LAST TWO MESSAGES FROM DR. CHOI'S secretary who called twice in two days to reschedule my session. I examined the receipt, lying on top of my keyboard, carefully. Ashley's dress cost more than my shoes and accessories, and with only thirty-seven dollars left in my purse to last for the rest of the week, I decided to go in to work early to pick up some extra hours.

"Okay, Melody, you'll have to be back before three o'clock," I said to the florid face standing in the doorway of my office. I kicked my Baker's shoebox underneath my desk.

"Can we make it at four?" Melody asked.

Her plum-red hair hung to her shoulders and a spray of freckles spread across her face. She held her hand on her middle like any average sixteen-year-old would.

"No. you can't."

"But I have things to do."

"We all do," I said, "but you know the rules. Miss a curfew and there will be serious consequences."

"What time are you off today, Rachel?" she asked.

I dropped the ink pen to direct my attention on her.

"Oops! I mean, what time are you off today, Ms. Rachel? I forgot," she said with a giggle.

"Maybe I'll be off before you get back, or maybe I won't," I said.

"But, I've never missed curfew."

"I wish I could help," I said, "but class ends at two-fifteen in the afternoon and that's giving you more than enough time to get back here before curfew."

"You guys suck!" Melody exclaimed, throwing herself against the door like a two-year-old having a tantrum.

"It's not fair," she whined.

"Sorry," I told her.

"No fair!" Melody stormed out.

I let the new pair of silver shoes I ordered for the wedding drop on top of the desk. The strapless white pumps had crystals glued to the heels and tips. I wiped my finger over the soft leather

106

that bridged across the heel of the shoe. They were sure to go really nice with my dress.

"Can I talk to you for a minute?" Michelle, one of the teen residents, asked as she positioned herself by the door.

I threw the shoebox back under my desk, and straightened my blouse before giving her my undivided attention.

"Sure, what's up?" I asked, fully prepared to hear another whiney teenager's problem.

Michelle let herself in and shut the door behind her. She sat on the edge of the chair and rocked back and forth. Her pale skin was almost jaundiced, and her long, thin hair blended in with her skin.

"Are you okay?"

"My period didn't come," she said.

The words crashed like china on top of my desk. The youthful voice of the child sitting across from me threw me for a loop as she fumbled with the tissues over her face. She dabbed her left eye while the right one looked at me for relief.

I sat there, frozen by her candor, in sheer agony. That was exactly what I felt when I realized two months after my naïve visit to Kareem's, that an intruder had invaded my body. Alone, and feeling trapped by shame, I was tormented, embarrassed and abandoned, but that wasn't the worst of it.

No. That came when Bethanny drove me to a clinic and reassured me she'd take care of everything. But once Pastor found out I was spreading my thighs wide for a female with a vacuum cleaner to suck out every life form from inside me, that plan was foiled.

"Are you having sex?" I asked.

I felt like I was Dr. Choi's assistant for a moment, but with genuine concern for my patient.

She wagged her head.

"What are you going to do?"

"I don't know," she replied, dropping her head between her knees, "what am I supposed to do?"

The hairs on my arms bristled for an answer, but I didn't push myself for one. The weight of my own guilt held me back, and my own actions for allowing such a thing to happen sent my pulse on a speed race. My heart began beating faster than hers.

107

"Well," I said, "what then?"

Michelle closed her fist under her chin and answered, "Not sure."

Fear shot out like rocket balls over and over in my head. "No matter what you decide, I'll support you," I told her.

Michelle sat quietly. I picked a Kleenex off my desk before offering it to her.

"It's going to be all right," I reassured her.

Those were the words I wanted to hear once. I held her by the waist with her baseball cap tucked under my neck. I held her tightly to lift her up from her own dead weight. The weight that I'd been carrying on my shoulder for so many years. Her bubble gum perfume couldn't eradicate the shame of my own guilt. But it lifted me somehow.

"I don't want to get rid of it," she said.

And without hesitation, I answered, "You don't have to. You can do whatever you feel is best for you." With my eyes locked onto hers, I added, "I'll do whatever I can to help you."

CHAPTER 24 Cynthia

I RETURNED TO THE COUNTY COURT HOUSE as I usually did on weekday mornings for scheduled hearings, but this time, I decided I'd go look for James. I planned to find him for no other reason than to tell him I caught on to his game. I knew he took my telephone number to entice me, and make me want him. The trick was out. The cat was out of the bag, and his ploy to trick me could only work once. I was ready to expose him and educate him on what real women like me already knew: *we can't be swindled.* Whether they'd given him money, or he convinced them to do his dirty tricks, it wouldn't work on me. I was no sucker.

I intended to not be belligerent, hostile or confrontational, even. I would be peaceful, calm and direct. I'd wait until he gave me his first compliment, then I'd attack him for his lies. After his three o'clock appointment with his parole officer, he was sure to be here any minute.

I checked my rearview mirror. He didn't bother to call even after he pried my number out of my lips.

I played with the lobe of my ear while daydreaming about questions I intended to ask when I cornered him.

So you like to bully? Did they bully you in jail? You think your charming looks can get you anything, don't you?

As I placed my mental questions in chronological order, James's maroon Honda rattled around the corner before entering the parking lot. I waited a second so he wouldn't feel ambushed, and only sprang into action after his car door opened.

Clenching the sleeve of my sweater closer to shield my skin from the wind, my curls blew opposite to where I directed them. Cars whizzed by, but it didn't matter because my focus was exclusively on putting James to shame.

He walked briskly towards the courthouse and I followed. The knot in my throat made it difficult to swallow.

"James," I said.

His shoulders broadened in his plaid, schoolboy shirt, and he suddenly wasn't as tiny as he appeared before.

"Hey, James," I repeated. *Yeah you! You're the one I have a problem with.* He rolled his shoulders and stopped in the middle of the lot. His long lashes curled like my toes did once my soft spot has been compromised. His eyebrow slanted sharply.

"WHERE ARE YOU GOING?" I asked, pulling on my sweater to fortify my nerve that suddenly took a backseat. I threw some masculinity into my voice to remind me of my sheer anger at his sneaky behavior. He hurled his arms out and pulled me forward and I didn't resist.

"Hey you," he said before laying a wet one on the side of my cheek, that I didn't wipe off. Afraid of the tingling I often felt when he was around, I struggled to think. Every part of his face was in my full view, his white teeth and eyes were translucent with excitement. There were no signs that his act was going to let up. He gestured with his hands from him to me.

"I got the job I wanted!" he exclaimed. "At a hospital! I need to talk. Me and you." He backed away from the scene of the crime, adding, "I have to see my probation officer," as if all were forgiven.

I stood in the middle of the lot and waited for someone to hit me. "We need to go out," he said. Raising his right hand to mimic holding a phone to his ear, "I'm going to call you."

I listened. I didn't move, and smiled like a teenager with a crush, while wishing I could kick myself in the butt.

"You free tonight?" My palms weren't sweaty, but my midsection was.

"You're tricking me," I said in a low voice, more for myself than for him to hear.

"What?" he shouted as he moved into the building. "I'm calling you tonight. And I want you to answer!"

He nodded his head, indicating for me to follow, and I shamefully said without any hesitation, "Yes." My throat felt like an urn of ashes, but it didn't stop me from yelling across the black paved lot, "I'll be waiting."

He stepped behind the automatic doors until I could only see his shadow. I walked back to my car without uttering a word, but felt humiliated by my own actions. There was something about James, or something James did that made me fall for his obvious trickery.

CHAPTER 25 BETHANNY

SITTING ON THE TOILET IN MY bathroom, I was holding our framed wedding photos while I contemplated what to do next. I was too ashamed to come out of the windowless, closet-sized pit I lived in, fearing my own shadow would be outside the door to confront me.

There was no way I could change anything that happened the previous night even though I wished I could.

On the day when Alex and I married, the vows I took before the woman officiating and God were of no importance, and held no more significance than if I'd recited them to myself.

"'Til death do us part," I said on that fateful day five years ago. Sharon stood on one side of me and my mother on the other. Those words meant more to me than the typical wedding ritual, and were required to make a marriage ceremony worth sticking around for. Alex was my provider, friend, lover, and anything else over the sun and moon. My marriage meant more to me than anything else. It even held more weight than my parents' desertion of me when I needed them; and I let everything that hurt me in the past go. I hadn't looked or touched another man since that day because the promise I made was to never allow anyone else to get between us.

The woman Alex cheated on me with and the two-hundred-fifty-pound body that was now snoring on my bed beside me sure snuffed that promise away.

I shouldn't have gone out with Sharon. I knew what everyone would say. *"He left that whore because she was sleeping around,"* or *"Can't turn Bethanny into a wife."*

I shouldn't have drunk so much, or brought him into my house, where my kids sleep, or into my husband's bed even though he abandoned it. I bit my hand after clenching it into a fist.

I had to get this man out of my house. What if Alex showed up? It was already light out and my nosy neighbors would surely see him. What if I were picking my kids up from Alex's, or his mother's, and they could smell the scent of sex seeping from the hairs of my skin? *Where'd he park his car?* Every time I felt ready to lift myself from the toilet seat, my legs became too heavy to support the weight of my body and pulled me back down.

Would Alex realize I didn't text him this morning, or beg him to come home as I'd done for the past week? Would he finally break down and run back to me? Maybe he would come to his senses. But not if he walked right into Laurent's naked body on his white sheets. The same sheets that were on our bed since he left me.

That wasn't in the plans. I thumped my knees to keep from bursting into tears, and took a few short breaths to help slow the pace of my pounding heart. I felt sickened by my weakness. Especially to a man I didn't even know. Haunted by my actions, I felt incredibly confused, and at the same time, unsure of where to lay blame. *He started this. Did he feel guilty?*

I beat on my chest to ease the hyperventilation, and only let up to sob some more. My marriage was over and so were my promises.

CHAPTER 26 Naomi

IT WAS ONE O'CLOCK IN THE morning and I could hear Cynthia toying around on the phone. She kept stopping in mid-sentence, like she was discussing something important. "Yes," she said, "he kissed me on my right cheek."

It's not like I could have slept with a balloon squeezed between a twin mattress and me. Crumbled paper lay scattered in the corner of the bedroom from the brilliant idea I had to convince Momma to change her mind about the wedding. The wedding day countdown had officially begun. It moved faster than I wanted. The only thing I could think to do was write, and I did. I wrote a letter to Momma:

Dear Momma,

Norman's not the man of my dreams. Quite frankly, I'm not the woman of his either. We've decided to remain friends to support our ~~daughter~~ child, so with your grace and blessings, I respectfully ask you to accept this letter from me to cancel the wedding.

Amen,

Naomi,

I read over it a few times and didn't think it'd get her attention. So I balled that one up and wrote another:

Dear First Lady Crieur,

Momma, I know you've been the greatest mother ever. You and Daddy want the best for us and I will show you how much you mean to me; just let me prove it. Let's cancel the wedding and I'll go back to school full time and become the registered nurse you always dreamed I could become.

Love,

Your youngest blessing.

I crumpled that one and figured it was no use 'cause Momma wouldn't read it. This wedding meant too much to her. She had a lot invested in it, including dignitaries who would finally keep all gossip about the Crieur family name from slipping through their lips. Pastor could resume his sermons on premarital sex and Momma could stop wearing black, or mourning over her youngest daughter's failures.

Norman would somehow make me a better woman, or so they surmised. They expected me to become a better person than I'd ever been before. If only Momma knew how hard it was to suck it up and carry his slack.

Maybe if I called him and said, "Changing diapers isn't a woman's job; I don't want to be the only one doing that, Norman!" Surely, that would easily turn into an argument that forced his hand to demand the wedding be canceled, thereby ending our troubles.

I definitely didn't want my Jessa knowing her momma wasn't good enough for her daddy. Momma wasn't good enough for Pastor either, but she hung in there because she learned to take whatever he threw at her, which was more often bad than good.

I didn't want any bad. It wouldn't do me any good.

Cynthia was laughing a lot in there. At least, someone found something funny. She could, at least, do and say what she wanted without being condemned for it. I guess that was because she was a big shot lawyer, whose lip service never needed any defense. That's probably the reason why she was exempt from my parents' constant criticism. I put a pillow over my head to shield my ears from Cynthia's trumpeting voice.

I'd have liked to tell her to tone her voice down, but I knew she'd say, while pointing to her front door, "There's a lot of silence out there." And I'd have to take my bubble gut and bubble butt back to Momma's, to endure the maximum sentence for disobeying. She'd just have given me more speeches and rules and even more reasons why I "needed to listen."

Cynthia clicked on the radio almost as quick as Jessa slammed me with another kick. These walls were too thin.

"There's something about him," Cynthia said to whomever was on the other end of the phone.

I pressed the pillow harder over my ear, hoping to block out her voice. *Shut up already.* I needed to refocus.

"Yes, girl!" Cynthia's voice streamed into my tidy room. "I'm going to see him."

I wished I could have stolen her joy for a moment. If only to make me feel for once like a person instead of a marshmallow dough girl with a wedding and baby on the way. The more I wrapped the pillow around my head, the more her joyful banter stung my ear.

Jessa's jagged punches sent me rolling onto my back. I tossed the pillow under my head and welcomed the deadly silence. Staring into darkness, I slipped into the peaceful sounds of nothingness. I rubbed the top of my belly to coax me back into a deep sleep, but the bass from Cynthia's juke-box started to blare, and stopped any calmness that I might have had left in me.

CHAPTER 27 ANDRE

SHIRLEY DIDN"T TAKE THE RESTRAINING order news too well. We'd been in the car, waiting on Scooter for the past half hour, and she hadn't stopped cursing to herself in the passenger mirror. "I should have slit her tires," Shirley muttered. The whites of her eyes were pink, and her lips smacked as often as she blinked.

I fibbed a little. I told her I had to turn myself into my probation officer this weekend and couldn't go to the wedding. I hoped that would keep her out of the church premises on the day of Naomi's wedding. That's all I needed. For her to show up and catch me in the act.

I needed a hit. I hadn't had any since I left Monique's, and Shirley's threats about Cynthia kept getting me uncomfortably excited.

"I'm going to knock her teeth out," she said.

I didn't respond because if I'd had a chance, I'd have kicked her teeth in too.

Cynthia seemed to forget she was my sister. She was supposed to have my back in all this, but she kept treating me as if I were a stranger. Family doesn't do family like that. She thought because she earned all of those college degrees, she was smarter. She thought she knew best. Well, she didn't. I'd tell her that too, if those thin sheets of paper she filed against me would allow me to approach her.

Shirley pounded her makeup brush on her cheek while she rambled. "I'm going to get fired if you go to jail, Andre," she said, "and then I'll *have* to kill her."

Then I'd have to find another place to crash every so often, since Monique keeps acting out again. She seems like she wants to give me her buns to kiss. I'm going to let her shine for a little while, just until after the baby, and then I'll see how much lip she gives me.

She was the reason I'd been staying at Shirley's house for a few days. I had to sneak through her back door so her mother wouldn't find me and all to keep from breaking Monique's neck. Shirley was doing her part right. She cooked, cleaned and kept me happy, because she knew just what it took.

I sensed the real reason Shirley was so worried. She knew if I were gone, she wouldn't get that good loving I liked to give her. I knew how to dice her up like fresh-picked tomatoes. She liked sitting on the edge of the bed as soon as I got out the shower, ripe and ready for Big Chopper to come handle her. I wasn't going anywhere, but I wouldn't tell the truth about that either.

Taking Shirley's hand, I rubbed the back of it while I looked her in the eye and wobbled my head in an effort to keep my somber face in place. "They're not going to give me more than a week," I said. "I can't imagine it being that bad."

The wrinkles in the corners of her eyes stretched out to her temples. "You think so, sweetie?" she asked.

Her eyebrows seemed to be in a tizzy with her eyes when she said, "Doesn't sound right." She shrugged and cracked each finger like she was breaking bread while keeping her eyes away from mine.

"I think that'll happen," I said, "So don't worry about losing your job or anything else. I'm pretty sure I'll be home in no time. " Shirley's body went up as she stared out the windshield of the car. "I mean, if court's on Monday," I said, "the judge should probably lock me up until Sunday."

Scooter came around the side of the building, seemingly unaffected by the heavy rain pitter-pattering on the hood of my car. The streetlight reflected off his bifocals as he took his usual position against the wall of the store.

I reached for the door handle, but released it as I turned to Shirley who just let out the waterworks. Tears ran down her face and I ignored them. Shuffling through my pants pocket, I handed her all that was left of what I found in Monique's purse. "Come on with that, Shirley," I said, "It's going to be all right. He's here now, so chill."

She jumped out of the car and ran like the rain were chasing her. Scooter didn't move from his post, but Shirley's hands waved around until she dropped them to her side. She opened her jacket and jumped up and down. Scooter pointed in my direction and I slid down in the seat to keep from locking eyes with him. I nervously slammed the wheel of the car and sunk deeper after the horn chimed in. Shirley walked back to the car with slumping shoulders and dropped herself in the seat. "He says you have to pay up," she said, "and he's not going to let us go."

What? Doing my best to catch my breath, the pain from my stomach festered and every word out of her mouth sounded like a lie. Scooter wouldn't send her back empty-handed. *All I needed was one for tonight.*

"I told him I don't get paid until tomorrow and he says to come back then."

Looking back at Scooter, who used his hood as a shield, I thought, *I can't wait. I need a hit now.* Zeroing in on Shirley, I saw her skirt had skated up to nearly her thigh, and her blouse was open with her chest half out. She must've slipped the white somewhere in there.

She was lying.

Flip-flops on her ashy feet and her purse still in the car, there was nowhere she could have hidden it. I suspected she got some, but wasn't sharing. *Greedy trick.* Scooter wouldn't leave me hanging like that though. I knew it. If I asked him if he gave her any white, he'd ask for his money. I didn't have it. I looked at Shirley who was back at the mirror, inspecting every part of her lying face.

I slapped the passenger side mirror closed and pushed Shirley's neck down onto the seat. "Where is it?" I demanded, "I know he gave you some."

Shirley punched my arms and I held my fingers around her neck. She looked like she was trying to keep from crying. I wouldn't let her go. I had to show her she should never try to play me for a fool. I sealed my elbows under her neck and repeated, "Where is it?"

I loosened my arms a bit to hear her say the words I already knew. She struggled and kicked her legs around the car like she was trying to get out. I pushed down on her neck harder.

"With all this stuff going on? With my sister trying to get me locked up?" I said. The whites of her eyes flushed red, and I loosened my grip to give her another chance to spill.

She panted. Sucking in the September air, she began to scream about everything except my white. I looked over at Scooter who lit a cigarette and made smoke clouds with the force of air exiting his mouth. I loosened my grip again to give Shirley another chance to dig out the white from her hiding place.

"Where is it?" I repeated louder.

She tossed her skirt pocket inside out, but I didn't move until she said, "He only gave me enough for me."

Her black bra was dangling out of her shirt, and she slipped her hand under the bra cup before extending the hand that held the white. I wrapped my hands around her head and kissed the middle of her forehead. She slapped the tiny bag into my hand as I got back in my seat.

"I'm sorry, baby," she said.

"With all the stuff I'm going through, baby," I said, "I just need you to support me no matter what." Her girlish looks shriveled as quickly as she wiped her eyes. Shirley cried and stopped only to hiccup like my baby sisters did when Momma left them in the crib too long.

"I'm about to go to jail," I said. Shirley let her glassy eyes take a break on me as she looked at me for a way out. "And I'm giving you all my time, and this is how you repay me?"

The hiccups stopped and so did her tears. She held onto the silence for a few minutes before wiping away the dampness in her cheeks. "I know I screwed up," she said, "and I'm going to visit while you in jail."

I took my eyes off her and plowed my hands into my pockets. Kicking the gas, I drove away.

CHAPTER 28 Pharah

SOMEONE FINALLY SHOWED INTEREST in me. I wasn't as excited as I was now, after receiving the email response from the dating website. It came from a man who called himself Nile. *Nile*, like a river, the north-flowing river of great Africa, *Hey Nile, will you marry me?*

Nile Jenkins, his profile said. He was a banker at some small company in Center City. I couldn't stop grinning after waking up with the knowledge I had an impending date. I was practicing my smiles after we'd officially met. He sounded awfully excited about my activities with the church, and I was equally impressed with his. He said he sings at his church choir and volunteers his time at local kitchens. We agreed to get together tonight.

We planned to meet at Rickey's Roast for a cup of coffee, which I thought was an ideal choice for a first date. It was cozy, quiet and private. The only problem was choir rehearsal. I couldn't back out of rehearsals with the wedding in only a few days, but I couldn't help wondering if I'd finish in time to meet up with Nile.

I stood behind the podium with my fist under my chin.

"What's wrong with you?" asked Raymond, one of the only choir members who truly could claim he had a voice.

"Nothing," I said, "nothing."

I had a hard time staying focused when I imagined Nile next to me. *How would I react? What would he think of me?* His profile placed him between thirty and thirty-five. Brown skinned, and in good shape, he appeared to be a good first pick. I fixed my shirt collar and flipped through the choir songs to make sure we were all on the same page.

"If this is how we're singing this weekend, guys" I said, "we shouldn't sing at all!" The twelve female and eleven male choir members were standing on the stage of my father's church.

"Come on, Pharah," Raymond said, "we've been at this all day. Maybe we should come back in the morning." He groaned and his pallid teeth looked as perfect as his smooth, brown skin, and hair that he twisted in locks. Talented with a commanding presence, he appealed to sinners like me and unknowingly provided enjoyment. *God, forgive me for my lustful heart.*

Raymond was a native of Haiti, and his Haitian accent sounded smooth to my ears. Even his stubby hands didn't bother me, because I knew how to put them to good use whenever I needed help from time to time at the church. He never mentioned if he were dating, or if he were even straight. But there was no way that bar of chocolate sexy didn't have someone to play house with. I let his image of my prince disappear long ago after he told me how "women came after" him, and he didn't "go after women."

I let him have that. I may have been in need of a husband, but I dared not be a thirsty one. I still considered him a friend. We spent time together during choir practice, and he'd been around long enough to know if something was bothering me even though he was testing me now.

"In the morning?" I said. "Raymond, the ceremony is this weekend!"

I stopped to rub the bottom of my throbbing feet, my punishment for taking advantage of them for the past nine hours. I thought wearing a new pair of shoes might make the date run more smoothly.

"Our voices should be well rested by then," he said. He towed a chair over to sit.

"Get up!" I said.

"Well, I'm tired.

I reeled in my eyes and pointed for him to stand. "Well, you need not sing in that case." Singing was a job that, if done right, could be healing. I took my job seriously and wished they would too. I clapped my hands to get the rest of the group moving. "Let's take it one more time," I said.

"His eyes are on the spar-row..." sang the choir.

"And I know," I sang. I moved my hand and gestured to the choir to follow me.

"And I know now," Raymond, my lead singer sang.

"He watches me," the choir chorused.

"All right, guys, we can meet here on Saturday morning; and no later than eleven a.m. I prefer you guys come dressed so you won't be late," I said.

The choir scattered out of the church, and Raymond took his seat again while I gathered my belongings. "Your hair looks cute," Raymond said, toying around with his phone. Excited, I teased the back of my hair. If he noticed it, so would Nile.

"Where'd you get it done?" he inquired. I gave him a *why do you want to know* look, and he laughed.

"Hair Expressions," I said, my eyes glued to my hand-held mirror. "Do you really like it, Raymond, or are you teasing?"

"It does look nice," he said. "I didn't know you went to the hairdressers very often," he added.

He didn't know I went to the hairdressers very often? Well, what was he trying to say? Did my hair always look bad? And would this date finally get to see a real nice hairstyle even though Raymond had no idea I was going on a date?

I remained quiet since I was in the house of the Lord and continued to tease my hair while ignoring Raymond's unusual insult. It was just what I should have expected from a man who thought a woman's only place was in the kitchen. I did my best to avoid revealing my dismay as I snatched my handbag,

"Let's get out of here," I said, "I have somewhere to be."

Raymond stood up and tapped his side and asked, "Can you drop me off on Fifth Street?"

Without question, I knew I'd be late for my date now.

CHAPTER 29 Rachel

I PICKED ASHLEY UP AN HOUR EARLY FROM her sitter. I brushed her hair into two pigtails while my hands shook. The thought of seeing Bruce again had me on edge. It only took one phone call to Bruce earlier today and he answered on the first ring, "Do you want to see your daughter in a couple of hours?" I asked.

It's one of the only times when I wished my impulsive behavior had vanished into the wind.

It didn't take him long to say "Yes, we'll meet at your mother's."

I lay Ashley's flowered dress out on the bed that matched her black patent-leather shoes. I tucked three of her jeans that shrunk overnight into the Macy's bag that I stacked against my bedroom door for Michelle's unborn, to begin the commitment I made to her even with the struggles of raising Ashley.

I made every effort to show Ashley off to the father who remained absent from her life more often than not. I tried to ensure I left no signs that my nerves were getting the best of me. By the time I headed to Momma's house, I made one small adjustment to our plans. "Bruce's behavior will dictate his future visits."

I was not sure if I should have been concerned at all, since so many years had passed and he may have already become a better man. Or a better person, for that matter. He could easily have made a complete three-sixty during his years of incarceration. Perhaps he was a different person now, and someone I could trust. Ashley could finally get to know him. Maybe he'd be so much better off that we could resume our relationship again.

Stop, just stop, Rachel! Scratch that thought. It can't happen. I was not ready for more drama.

I parked in front of my parents' house and had a good grasp of the steering wheel in the hand that wouldn't stop shaking. Everything was now planned, but I couldn't help but think I may have made a mistake. Tucking my hand between my armpits, I discovered my shirt was already drenched from an abundance of perspiration. My scalp itched from its dampness, and my breathing wasn't too regular either.

Momma's rose shrubs in her yard were neatly aligned in a row, like militia in an army, and I thought that was to mirror the stillness. The thought of Bruce going over my head and making matters worse, as well as Pastor's speech about visiting his church, took their prominent places inside my head too. Looking around the passenger side of my car for a paper bag, (a calming remedy from Dr. Choi's pamphlets), I got an uneasy urge to run. The bubble of fear was fast approaching and I could no longer ignore it.

Take a deep breath, Rachel. In and out. In. Then just out.

I blew as hard as I could, in my own hands, but it didn't work.

In and out. Nothing. *In and out.* Take a deep breath, Rachel Crieur.

Closing my eyes, I tried it again, *in and out.*

"I want to get out," Ashley yelled from the back seat, but I couldn't stay focused long enough to register it.

Okay, think of Ashley. She's your baby and she won't hurt you. Don't break down in front of her. Deep breaths. In and out.

My chest pounded, but I slowly got a grip on it. I searched for something else to calm the demon that grabbed hold of me.

There's nothing to be afraid of, Rachel, said my normal, sane self to the crazy twin. *It's all in your head. Hold the wheel.* SO I DID. *In. Out.*

Too fear-stricken to move, I held the air tightly in my chest while struggling to breathe and stay awake.

Breathe. I opened my mouth to suck air in since it wouldn't go in on its own. I couldn't hear Ashley anymore because everything was in slow motion and mute. I tried, but I couldn't. It didn't work. I stopped fighting and was ready to throw in the flag when my car door was suddenly flung open and I saw Pastor's hands extended.

CHAPTER 30 Cynthia

BY THE TIME I SAT DOWN at Ricky's Roast Restaurant, I had all but scrapped the idea of confronting James about how he slicked his way into stealing my phone number. I chose a more fitting punishment: arrive more than a half hour late and act unimpressed. I'd gone back and forth between feelings of extreme anger and extreme confusion, all within minutes apart. I purposely left my sunglasses in the car so my partially blackened eye would suggest that I was a fighter. I didn't comb my hair or wear makeup and threw on my old, navy sweat pants.

I thought if we made a truce tonight, we could potentially begin a fresh, new friendship. Then I could go back to living my normal life without James's conniving tactics. The restaurant wasn't very fancy. The checkered red and white tablecloths made the room feel homey. The music was stationed to some old classical stuff, and to my surprise, he was seated at our table in the middle of all the hungry men and women. He was even wearing a tie as if he were going to a special event. His khakis were ironed, and judging by the firmness of his polyester shirt in the shoulders, it had obviously been steamed to rigid perfection.

He sat in a corner nearest the back and gave me one of those *I see you, girl* little smirks. His hazel eyes boasted his confidence. They resembled an expression of one who just accepted an offer on a date. But I was prepared. I was ready to challenge his calculating abilities to swing things around to his favor. I was ready for any of his games because he obviously didn't know what type of person he was dealing with.

I had no plans to discuss his kids or his income, I just intended to take a moment and re-establish a friendship, or another avenue of mutual respect between adults. Our paths wouldn't cross, and we weren't heading the same direction since he didn't want the same things in life that I did.

He stayed on cue, and did his usual immediate hugs, perhaps for a second longer than the last time. There were no telltale signs or scents of illegal drugs in the air, and I wished that was how we started off from the beginning. I was gladly willing to make him feel important if that was what he wanted since I was really good with words.

"Sorry to keep you waiting," I said as genuinely as I could. I slithered my baggy sweat pants into the cushioned seat while our eyes met.

"It's okay," he replied, adding, "you look *beautiful*."

I thought of giving him the *you have to be kidding me* speech to signal that his compliment was weak. I eventually evicted the words from my brain, however, so the idea didn't linger long enough to stick.

"How was your day?" he asked.

What the heck do you think? You should know! You've been occupying my mind all day. "Fine," I replied.

Holding the menu far enough from my face to shut him out of it, I skimmed through the wine section 'cause Lord knew I was in dire need of something to help me unwind. I felt his eyes luring me with his conniving, sneaky hook. I was saved by the pretty waitress who stood across from me. Her gray eyes were friendly and devoted to James. No less than a D-cup bra size, her hair fell down to her waist, but I was not sure if it was all hers. She flipped her white pad out of her back pocket and asked, "Are you ready to order, sir?"

James nodded his head, signaling for me to order first. A true gentleman, surprisingly.

"I'll have a drink," I said, "A Moscato, my favorite."

"Mine too," he concurred.

Surreptitiously swerving my head over at the waitress whose gaze was riveted on James, I thought, *Now, go away girl.* Mental note to girl: *He doesn't want you.*

The waitress walked away with our order and I thumbed through my thoughts for something to say. The silence between us was weird. He looked at me, and I glanced at him. Pulling out my phone, I placed it on the table and he did the same. To cut the awkwardness, I took the salt and pepper bottles on the table and began to imitate my own personal drum. I tapped to the tune of U2's "We Will Rock You." James put both his elbows on the table and turned me into the focal point. "Do I make you nervous?" he asked.

I collected my thoughts, while trying not to abort my original plan to avoid being suckered. Crossing my fingers, I jammed them behind my back and glided my chair closer to the table so he could hear me clearly.

"No," I said, "there's nothing about you that makes me nervous."

Judging by the grin on his face, James wasn't buying it, so I kept my eyes on him and did my best not to blink.

He moved his tongue over the arched part of his upper lip, and tossed his tongue inside of his mouth all around as if in a struggle. His hair was freshly cut and his warm eyes saluted me. He brushed his hand over my face. And I, Cynthia Crieur, became hypnotized by the soft tenderness of his caress. Yet the faint screams of "GET OFF ME, YOU TRICKSTER! GET OFF!" created a battle inside my head.

"So if I do this…" he said like an airplane ready to land, as he shifted towards me and planted his lips squarely on mine. He tapped them ever so lightly and I didn't stop him. His eyes closed, but mine wouldn't. Ten, nine, eight, seven, six, and I did *it*. I slipped my tongue into his mouth to torment him for bullying me. I grabbed my hand from across the table and just let go. I let it all go.

He yanked himself away and I retreated. I kept looking around the room as if he and I were naked. My hands were still in his, and he rubbed the tips of my fingers. I was now more convinced than ever that James was making things much more complicated.

CHAPTER 31 Pharah

I WOULD SURELY BE LATE because of Raymond! I locked the doors of the church and made believe Raymond's worried look didn't exist. He checked his phone sparingly for the bus schedule. "Where's your car?" I asked, somewhat annoyed by his bad timing.

"The shop," he said, "needs service."

Peeking at the time again, I was already eleven minutes late, and Nile was probably frustrated with me. He probably won't care to have a solid discussion about our views on marriage and faith because, for all he knew, I was an habitually tardy person. I'd waited months and years for a single moment with someone who'd be there for me, and now this?

I wiped the sweat from my neck while Raymond tried to give me a guilt trip when he said, "I'm only a block from the Roast." Curving his lips, he clarified his comment, "Main Street."

"Rickey's Roast?" I jumped on it so I wouldn't feel as bad leaving Raymond on the steps of the church despite his unnecessary observations.

"Yeah," he said, "going to see a friend of mine."

Just as I suspected, it must've been a woman friend. Even Raymond had someone. Someone was waiting on him, LIKE ME, for once, and I couldn't get there fast enough. I hopped in my car and said, "Put your seat belt on," while pushing down the gas pedal like I had somewhere important to go.

"If you're in a rush," Raymond said, "I can probably get the bus from here."

Great, now you tell me when I'm barely three blocks away!

"It's fine, Raymond."

"I see you got your nails done too, huh?" he said. I drew my fingers away from his sight and glanced his way.

"Really Raymond?"

"What?" he asked with a sneer on his face.

"Yes," I said, "I had a manicure. I was due for one."

"When'd you start getting manicures?"

Raymond had never given me anything but a useful hand, and only when in need, but tonight he was putting his foot where it didn't belong. I had to get over to my date, who probably thought I abandoned him. "Look, Raymond," I said, "my nails are always done. Besides, it's my sister's wedding in a few days. Can you be quiet over there?"

"OKAY," he replied, raising both hands above his head. "They look really pretty."

I sped through the intersections with Nile in mind. Weaving in and out until I spotted the double-parked car in the middle of the road. *YIKES! TRAFFIC!*

I averted my eyes when the smile on his face turned my stomach.

"Just let me out right here," he said, and I didn't hesitate when he closed the door shut behind him. He wound his fingers to gesture that I should roll down my window, so I did. "Have fun tonight," he said, "and I'll see you at rehearsal dinner tomorrow."

I began to slam on my brakes, but didn't. "RAYMOND," I yelled out as he stuck his hands in his pocket and briskly walked into the cold.

"Yeah?" he replied as he spun around.

"My mother's house; I'll need help with the favors."

"You got it," he said.

By the time I pulled into the parking lot of the restaurant, I was afraid of what I would find inside. The lot was full, and I was sure there'd be people running all around, staring at me and wondering why I came all alone. Then I'd have to explain to the maître d how I got stuck in traffic on my way, which caused me to be too late and, no doubt, made my date leave.

Drawing down the mirror of the car, I checked my makeup and added a few lines here and there. Dear Lord, if I was meant to be with Nile, everything will be good, and he'll still be here. Smell check: breath, check. Armpits, still dry. Hair, check. Then again.

Strolling inside the restaurant, I pressed hard on my new kicks, and said, "Table for Mr. Nile, please?" to the maître d. Taking one last breath before I made an outstanding impression, everything appeared to be in order, and I knew he was near.

"I'm sorry, ma'am," she said, "but there's no reservation by that name."

I could easily have run out of there and she'd never have noticed. Or pretend my hair, nails, eyelashes, and makeup never happened, but my shoes couldn't handle it. I made a mental note to pull up my big girl panties as I took a nice, big gulp. Looking around, I decided to play make believe. "I'm sorry, miss," I said, "I must be in the wrong restaurant."

I smiled. Yes, I smiled to keep from crying and continued making the rounds with my eyes. Then, deep in the corner, under a dimmed light I saw my sister, Cynthia! Her hair looked unkempt, but she was clinging to a man. *A man!* Dear Lord. A thug. No. A client. No. A man who was driving his tongue down her throat!

Chapter 32 Rachel

JUST WHAT I NEEDED: FOR BRUCE TO make me look like the worst mother ever. He was the source of all my anxieties. He was ruining my life. Drawing my damp hair into a ponytail since my curls had disappeared, Momma thought hosing me down with cold water might snap me out of the trance.

Cold, wet, and bewildered, I sipped the cup of tea she now set in front of me. Momma didn't say much and I didn't either.

Elsie stepped into the kitchen with a cell phone attached to her ear. "You okay, sweetie?" she asked. Her hair was wrapped in a black, silky scarf and she was dressed in a two-piece pajama suit.

"I'm fine," I answered.

My hands shuddered so I was quick to revert to my cup of tea, which bought Elsie enough time to back out of the kitchen. Momma was seated across from me and not doing much of anything. She got up from the chair every so often to check on Ashley and came back with another look of sincere concern.

Pastor hadn't shown his face since he shoved me in the house. I imagined my episode would have been too much for him because of the neighbors. I couldn't explain why it happened. I didn't know the reasons for it myself.

Taking a last gulp of the tea before I felt strong enough to face her, "Momma," I said over the crackle in my voice.

Momma's chin hung down and the corners of her lips bunched together.

"Did Daddy help me out of the car?"

Momma didn't utter a word, but continued cooking in the kitchen. I'm sure it was he. Not sure though if he knew it was me in the car.

I got up and pushed the kitchen chair back in.

"Her dad should be here any minute," I said. Moving about the open kitchen, I heard Pastor's voice coming from the living room.

"How are you?" Pastor asked, presumably to Elsie. I tiptoed to the door of the kitchen and pretended to gather up dishes, but was eager to hear how much admiration Pastor could dole out to someone besides me. Maybe it was one of his neighbors who dropped by, snooping to know what the commotion was all about. Or perhaps he was trying to practice *HOW TO PRETEND LIKE YOU ARE A CONCERNED INDIVIDUAL.* Looking toward Momma, who was wearing another one of her muumuus, I wanted answers, but she shrugged like she was minding her own business. The seriousness in her face was unmistakable so, to avoid rekindling my panic, I stood still for a minute.

"Who's he talking to, Momma?" I asked, somewhat hesitant to join him.

"Your mommy's going to be okay," Pastor said to his guest.

YOUR MOMMY'S GOING TO BE OKAY? Maybe one of the church members stopped by for an urgent prayer. I scrapped the whole deep thought idea out of my head as I wondered where my child was in all of this?

"Momma? Is Ashley upstairs?"

Momma went about her work in the kitchen. She switched on one of her Sunday morning tunes, and hummed to the music. So I stepped out into the hall to listen.

"She's just tired," Pastor said, " but she'll be all right. She's a smart girl. She can take care of herself, just like she takes care of you."

I wished the person he was speaking to would reply. My nerves were bubbling again. Momma tapped me on my right shoulder, which temporarily quieted my nerves.

"Pastor, won't like it if you're fussing," Momma said, "so if your guest is still coming, keep your friend outside."

Just like Momma. She caught wind of my eavesdropping and was only trying to find an easy way out for Pastor. I did exactly as I wished and stayed mum.

The sound of the doorbell ringing sent my fingers into my mouth, and I munched away all that was left of my nails. Pulling down my peach flared skirt, I flattened my stomach and stormed into the room.

There was Pastor, and so was Ashley. Ashley held her thumb in her mouth, sucking on it like the nipple of a bottle while Pastor slid his hand over the side of her arm as if to calm her in his lap. Pastor was clinging onto my Ashley with his hand over her head as if in prayer. Ashley's brown eyes were watering, but they grew wide once I was in her sight, and she threw her arms out for me. I hurried to lift my baby from Pastor's arms without looking at him, if only to avoid another panic episode.

Pastor stood before me and asked, "Are you feeling better?"

I wouldn't look at him at first, and struggled to keep my eyes averted. I feared the demons of my attacks would reappear. But I glimpsed at him only once to show him I wasn't an evil sinner. I was not the person he was convinced I was. Once I saw his gray eyes without the usual redness between them, I kept my gaze on him. I just kept staring at him, eye-to-eye, like it was a secret match that took five years to end. The doorbell rang again, and I knew it was Bruce. Whether from my allergies or my nerves, I had to rub my eyes.

"I'm doing very well," I said.

Hurrying past him with Ashley in my arms, I went toward the door and asked, "Are you coming back in?"

"Yeah."

I was certain another attack would ensue and I waited by the door for it, but it never came. The floor beneath me didn't disappear either. I held onto Ashley who bobbed her head around to see behind the door.

PASTOR SPOKE TO ME! I almost dared myself to run into the living room and give Pastor a hug. A challenge to my soul. One I needed more times than I could count. But I sputtered like an old, beat-up Cadillac.

WAS IT ONE OF HIS RUSES? My focus changed from fear to excitement to… nothing. Not one nerve jumped when I swung the door open. I stepped out onto the landing of my parents' house where Bruce held a daisy next to his chest. I quickly stole a glance at Momma's neighbor's lawn to make certain Bruce hadn't visited it.

"Greetings," he said, rolling out his hand to Ashley. My mind wandered aimlessly with Pastor in it. Ashley was intrigued by the white petals, which she ripped out of Bruce's hand. "That's what Daddy bought for you," Bruce told her.

I didn't do anything; I stayed quiet. Mentally repeating the chain of actions from the moment I pulled into my parents' home, I pretended I was there with Ashley as an assistant and we were waiting for Bruce's questions. I stepped away in the distance to give them some time to catch up on the years he missed. I did the same, except I was thinking about Pastor. Ashley rolled the flower in her hand like dough, and smiled at Bruce. "It's gone," she said.

Bruce slapped his bald head and gave her a high five. The stars of admiration appeared in her eyes. Bruce walked over to me with a mellow smile, but I didn't know what to make of it so I stood more erect, and waited.

"She doesn't look like me," he said, keeping his hands on hers. Ashley tossed the flower up in the air and jumped in an effort to catch it.

She doesn't look like you. What? As in, she's not yours?

"She looks more like your side," he said, "got that cute smile."

"I think she does," I said. *Nothing looks as it seems, Bruce. She's clean, but fed? No, thanks to you!*

Closing my mouth to prevent the sourness from spreading, I tried to wrap my mind around Pastor. *Pastor must truly think I'm smart.* I struggled to keep these two men apart in my head, but Pastor was winning. *Was I too smart for Bruce?*

Bruce looked at me as if he knew what I was thinking. Neither of us said a word.

Bruce placed his cold hands on my waist, saying, "I missed you." I backed away and pointed to Ashley. Ashley pulled the last few petals from her flower.

"What?" he said, "and when are we getting married? Huh?"

I curled my lips and lifted them as close to the tip of my nose as possible so Bruce would know that thought wasn't being considered, *right now*.

"Ashley! Don't rip up the flower Daddy gave you, sweetie!" I shouted.

Bruce flagged my reprimand away as if he had more important things on his mind. "It's okay," he said, "let her go ahead and play." Pointing his long finger towards Ashley, he turned his attention my way. "We need to make it work for her."

I dug my hands deeply into the back pockets of my jeans. Shrugging my shoulders, I felt like I was in a struggle between good and evil. I heard my own lips making popping sounds to cut through the uncomfortable silence caused by Bruce's presence and words.

"Bruce," I said, "let's not talk about this right now."

Typical for Bruce, he wouldn't let up in his determination to keep the dream about us alive. I only wished he'd give as much thought on keeping a job.

"Then… when?"

He didn't let his eye wander away from me so I pressed my lips together until I heard them *pop*.

CHAPTER 33 Cynthia

I WAS BORDERLINE CRAZY AT THIS POINT, and I fully accepted that disclaimer. So did James who was nibbling on my fingers as if I were a course in tonight's meal.

"You want me to stop?" James asked, but I said nothing. I was not quite ready to admit that I'd crossed over. I was letting him win. I was actually giving in to the pressure coming from a minimum wage character from my former neighborhood. *Oh no!*

I wiggled my hand away, but James didn't let go. That failed to terribly upset me, however. I just wished I could have shaved off some of his criminal history, and possibly, a couple of the tattoos. It would be quite hard to make him presentable to my friends. I could get him a good paying job, and make it work, but that criminal record! James tugged on my hands again, and I put my worries on ice.

"What're you thinking about?" he inquired.

I wouldn't say. Unless he really wanted to hear the *I CAN"T DATE A CRIMINAL* speech. We'd already started out on the wrong foot, with his unsophisticated trap to get me here, and now I was at his mercy. Although I did enjoy every bit of his soft lips, and warmth, and curious stares that had me wondering if he were fantasizing about me.

"Starting a new job on Monday," he said.

I took that moment to snatch my hand back. Rolling my eyes, I briefly batted them and tried to conceal my need to avoid the unavoidable.

"Really?" I said, "That's nice; where?" *Please no fast food. Ugh, Cynthia. I'd have to scream.*

Observing the crowd in the restaurant, I crossed out anyone in my mind that could've recognized me.

"At a hospital, "he said, "cleaning operating room utensils."

A hospital! He'd have to wear scrubs, and hopefully, ones without color-coding. You know, red for cleaning staff, blue for nurses, and white for doctors, which would only result in more pressure and embarrassment for me. If anyone asked, I'd just say "in a hospital" and wonder if they'd ever know.

James's confidence was as big as the hole in my gut. He rubbed the hairs of his chin and played with my ring finger. "At the Jefferson Hospital in Center City," he said.

Dropping my hands on the table, I could feel sweat bubbles beading in and around my temple. "Jefferson?" I asked. And right then, the awful beeping sound from the information desk at Jefferson Hospital rang in my head. The constant request I used to make for the desk clerk to page "Dr. Terrance, and please let him know his girlfriend is here."

I'd always ask for the redheaded granny who certainly wasn't in any competition to get a good look at what Doc had in his hands. What will I now look like when I strut into the hospital lobby, clad in my Donna Karan suit, and demand the desk clerk page the janitor?

For Christ's sake!

Freezing the muscles in my cheeks into an appropriate smile, I swallowed a quick gulp and said, "Congratulations."

CHAPTER 34 Bethanny

I decided to spend an extra day scrubbing all the remnants of Laurent off my body. I ignored his relentless phone calls throughout the night to prevent suspicion before I picked my kids up from Ms. Ethel as I promised today. I was an hour early, and very careful to avoid giving any impression of impropriety. Ms. Ethel said, "You're still my daughter and no matter what happens, I'll be there for you."

I knew better. I planned to keep his mother on my side, hoping he'd eventually follow suit, but she was still HIS mother.

I asked her last night if she'd been in contact with Alex, and hoped that would reassure her that I still wanted my marriage to work. And she replied in a matter of fact voice, "No dear." Even though I knew she may have thought her son could do no wrong, I could not help visualizing her cramming her three hundred unapologetic pounds into her 1992 Honda Accord to look for Alex and his no-good girlfriend. "I'm not getting into the middle this one," she said before she hurried off the telephone and added, "I didn't raise my son that way, dear."

I parked my car on the neat street and walked across the evergreen manicured lawns, and the large patios, dodging the kids playing out on the driveways. I kicked the kink out of my leg before ringing her doorbell and waited a few seconds before ringing again. Peering through the bay window of the dining room where Ms. Ethel and my kids sat, I waved from behind the window, but Ms. Ethel didn't move an inch.

"I'M HERE TO PICK THE GIRLS UP!" I yelled through the thick, solid, double-paned framed view. Ms. Ethel was middle-aged with caramel-colored cheeks that she kept overly powdered red and eyebrows that curled like cat whiskers. Her head was wrapped in a towel and she was wrapped in her bathrobe. She hesitated a moment before giving me the "one minute" gesture as she arose from the sofa. I read her lips when she replied, "I'm coming."

I didn't bother to wait for her to let me in, since I'd waltzed in many times before without waiting. I turned the doorknob and stepped inside the cozy home, with a leather sofa, fresh flowers, and freshly painted white walls. I considered Ms. Ethel my favorite of the two "mothers-in-laws" as Alex called them, and she sure did put up a good front.

She said she "wished our marriage had lots more loving years," and offered to "take the kids for the weekend" so I could have a "date night."

The next thing for her to do was point Alex toward the way back home and that should all but do it; however, I was determined to be patient. I cased the living room and checked the photos and snapshots hanging on her walls, chronicling Ms. Ethel's most special moments. Scanning the fireplace mantel for my beloved, summer day's wedding picture, it was not where it usually was, which was in line with photos of our kids. Nevertheless, there was one lonesome picture in its place. It was of Alex between the ages of six and seven years old, with fat cheeks, that he later replaced with fat lies.

"I was going to bring them out to you, sweetheart," Ms. Ethel said. Her back was shaking as she marched herself up the stairs before stomping her way back down. "The kids are in there," she said and I watched Ms. Ethel's shadow disappear while I continued my inspection of her place.

Max ran up to me and stood by the flight of hardwood stairs with a big smile on his face, "MOMMY," he said, "I don't want to go yet." Drawing his curly hair away from his face, I kissed his naked cheeks, and welcomed his visible excitement. As small as it was, it was something I desperately needed.

"We have to go now, sweetie," I said, forcing out a sharp, higher pitch and adding, "WE HAVE TO VISIT GRANDMA AND GRANDPA, BABY."

I shared the news to Max, which I drummed up only seconds earlier so Ms. Ethel would convey it to her beloved offspring about how "Bethanny even visits her parents now," and "she's really trying; so you need to go back!"

At least, it was good news she'd be able to tell him once she finally got hold of him.

"We made airplanes," Max said, holding his cut-out airplane over his head. I wished I could fly away in it to a deserted island and reprogram the story of my life: first, a new set of parents that loved me for who I was. Then, a husband, a *real one* who wouldn't leave me. My kids would stay all the same, only Max's voice would be a little deeper; and for once in my life, I could put my former career of stripping behind me. Then no one could say, "She isn't worthy."

"Daddy helped me with my airplane!" Max's jovial smile couldn't keep my ears from working. Dropping down to eye level with the three-foot, gloating youngster I was careful not to damper his excitement.

I meshed my teeth together and asked in a soft voice, "Daddy?" My tone remained low and calm for the moment.

Max jumped up with the airplane in his hand like my saying "Daddy" was his permission to let his excitement escape. "Daddy says he's going to buy me more airplanes when we move in with his GIRLFRIEND," Max said.

His three-foot size suddenly swelled into a mean-hearted giant.

"Don't say that!" I yelled as I yanked the airplane from Max's hand and leveled it against the fresh, white walls.

"NO, MOMMY," Max protested.

He dropped all of his weight on the floor and kicked the air while he was down there. Ms. Ethel took her time coming down the stairs, with my remaining troops following close behind. I didn't hesitate to take her on a Friday afternoon challenge.

"So you *have* been in contact with him?" I said. "You're nothing but a liar, Ms. Ethel." I threw my words out like daggers, which I aimed at her chest and she instinctively held her hand over it.

"What are you talking about, child?"

"You know what I'm talking about!" I fumed. "You know exactly what you're doing!" Ms. Ethel heaved in and out like I'd struck more than a nerve.

"Has Alex been here?" She wasn't sharing. What kept her from mouthing the words? I already knew what the answer was. "Has he?" I repeated.

My voice cut through Max's screams of "DADDY!" which didn't subside even after I tossed the bits and pieces of his airplane back to him.

"Alex?" Ms. Ethel looked about the room as if she were unaware that she was his mother.

"Ms. Ethel," I said, "if he didn't want to be with me, why did he marry me?"

"You need to leave my house, dear," she said, "this is very petty." I held still and pled my heart out to her like she was a juror in my criminal case.

"I just want my family back."

Ms. Ethel threw up her wrinkled fingers as if she were ready to give me a scolding. Throwing her left hand on what was once her hips, she said, "If he wants you, girl, he'll come for you. It's just that simple."

"If he doesn't love us anymore, then it's his loss."

"Whom do you mean by us, dear?"

Ms. Ethel raised her head as high as it could go to meet my eyes, but her efforts were futile. As much as I would have liked to rid Laurent from my life, his message about his son resonated momentarily with me. I abandoned my plan to attack Alex's character and that of his mother, and settled on attacking his parenting.

"He hasn't called his children," I said.

"It's not time, dear." Ms. Ethel stayed resolute. She stepped down from the stairs and walked to her front door. Opening it, she said, "It's time to go home, dear."

I peeled Max off the floor and escorted the other two girls using my thumbs and index fingers. After flinging all three into the back seat of my car like bowling balls, I got into the driver's seat. Alex was not coming home. Ms. Ethel was not going to bring him home. Alex no longer wanted to be with me and that made me petty.

Ms. Ethel drew her curtains and I did my very best to restrain the flood of tears that anxiously waited to be released.

CHAPTER 35 Andre

I DUMPED EVERYTHING OUT OF MOMMA'S purse while she was downstairs entertaining. She was entertaining everyone. They were all there: Naomi, Rachel, Pharah, and Bethanny, everyone except Cynthia. Cynthia's absence was probably for the best. I wasn't sure how I'd react to her with all of my problems. And she was the reason Momma was on my back.

Cynthia was trying her best to send me away and Momma was making it seem like I was somehow responsible. All I asked her for was thirty dollars, and she went on and on about how I "needed a job to stay out of trouble," and I "screwed up, Andre," she whined. "The restraining order means that you can't go Naomi's wedding."

Good. Less confusion for Shirley and me.

Just like Momma to roll the dice whichever way she thought the wind was blowing that day. And the dice weren't rolling my way. She said she wanted me out of her house before her princess daughter, Cynthia, got there, so I took her advice. I planned to leave once I'd found enough coin to get a hit. She had a credit card-sized Bible, millions of bits of scribbled paper, and the bottom of her handbag was damp. I found a damp envelope stuck at the bottom of her bag, which was filled with cash and I stuffed it into my pocket. There wasn't anything about the family that made sense. She knew my struggles, that we were about to have another baby, and how hard I've been looking for a job. She knew I was stomping around town and applying for any rank, dink job just so I could get by, but it wasn't working. It wasn't like Pastor would break his neck to get me a job at the center.

Pastor wouldn't talk to me about anything, and now Momma was getting ready to follow suit. After today, I planned to just stay away altogether. Looking over my shoulder to make sure no one was looking, I took a few dollars from Pastor's suit jacket. I headed down the dark hallway, feeling my way for the banister as I thumped down the staircase, and there Momma stood. With her floral apron wrapped around her ample waist, she dropped her hands from her hips and blocked my escape.

"If you don't get help, I'm going to turn you in, Andre," she said.

Turn me in? My hands tumbled like rocks into my pockets and I made sure the envelope didn't slip out far enough for Momma to notice. Momma didn't know anything about what I did, and neither did my siblings. If she was speculating now, that meant one of those gremlins had been snitching. Monique wouldn't put my business out there, and Shirley? No, she was a rider. I cocked my head back in surprise at her inquiry.

"What are you talking about, Momma?"

"Andre," she said, "I'm going to the courthouse myself to tell the judge what you've been doing. I can't live like this anymore, Andre, you have to get some help."

I could smell the scent of Momma's rage burning. Her nose flared like a balloon. She looked torn between throwing a punch, or one of her crumpled Bibles at me.

"Get yourself some help, Andre," she demanded. Momma was not one to take lightly, especially when she was pissed, so I did like I was supposed to. I jumped to the left side of her, and she followed and quickly moved to the right.

"What have I been doing, Momma?" I said, "What?"

Grinding her teeth, her eyebrows rose like bread dough, and I wasn't prepared for the language that rolled off her tongue: "DRUG ADDICT, CRACKHEAD" and "USELESS, NO GOOD SON!"

I looked for an easy exit before her words caught up with me.

"BOOOYYYY?" she said. She planted her two hundred-pound, five-foot-one-inch body in front of me. I dodged right, and she moved left as I pounded my way out the front door into a recognizable stranger with a purple teddy in hand who stood outside the front door. His eyes kept blinking and his shoulders hung as low as his head. I stepped back for another glimpse.

"What's up, Andre?" he said. "Your sister in there?"

"You, huh?"

Hearing Momma's feet must have been part of her set-up, and she was swiftly making her way to the door, so I sped up my legs and ran straight out of there.

CHAPTER 36 Rachel

I THOUGHT IT WOULD BE NICE TO INVITE BRUCE back to Momma's house tonight after the dinner party ended. My belly was full and so was Ashley's.

"I'll be right back, Momma," I said after Bruce arrived. She and Pastor sat huddled on the living room sofa as if they were tuned into some mental game.

I casually walked by them and heard Pastor respond, "Okay."

Bruce and I walked Ashley around the block, hand-in-hand, to make her feel like we were still a family. I resisted at first, and was not ready to allow Bruce's unwavering determination to bring us back together to become permanent. I considered my options at length and was still on the fence about it all. I also considered the humiliation of repeated embarrassment.

He needs to be a father jumped out at me like a ghost. I did my part as far as including him until he decided it was too much. But I couldn't help hoping he would turn out to be everything I truly wanted. Maybe he was who he needed to be for me. Temporarily on a hiatus from Carson, even though my body craved him just about every day, I was beginning to miss our regular visits. But it gave me the chance to clear my head from everything. I still had no plans in place for Bruce, but intended to take things slowly.

He was dressed in a green hat and a green button-down shirt. He brought Ashley a teddy bear with purple letters that said, "I love you" on a tag around it. He was definitely trying, but I remained wary.

Probably stuffed the bear under his shirt as he walked briskly past the cash register. Can't really trust anything he says or does anymore.

However, he hadn't sworn as often and wasn't asking for me to do anything for him.

"So are you ready to give us another chance?" he asked, batting his eyelashes like a love-struck Cupid. Ashley was using Bruce's and my hands as her personal swing and she giggled after I let her down while Bruce zipped up his Timberland jacket to his neck. The ends of his blue jeans were rolled on top of the rims of his boots. He moved his head toward my face so he could take a closer look at me. I stopped in the middle of the sidewalk and wrapped my hand over Ashley's cold ears.

"Let's talk about that later," I said.

"Why not now?"

Now? I'm not ready to form a decision, and if I did, it would fall in line with everything else in my life when I failed. Failure is the product of impulsive behavior.

"Bruce," I said, "we're not there yet."

"When then?"

The weight of the world was balanced on my back. *Ashley's laundry wasn't done. I hadn't written next month's rent check, and there was approximately eleven dollars left in my bank account. Oh, and Bruce? You still owe me money.* I rubbed the back of my neck and sucked in the dry air for as long as I could.

"Bruce," I said, "ask me about you in another year."

"Yeah?"

"Yeah," I said.

CHAPTER 37 Bethanny

I needed to hide out somewhere safe, free from everything and everyone whose goal was to crack me. I did as I promised and stopped by my parents' house, and of course, it was the night of the rehearsal dinner.

Ms. Ethel's "petty," comment wasn't going to stain me because she didn't truly know the real me or what I did. I loved Alexus. More than she'd ever know. He cheated. He was a cheater. Did she tell her son he was "petty" for snubbing his wife and having an affair that would surely scar my sacred heart for life?

If there wasn't anything else in my life that needed cleansing, it was my heart. I also needed to cleanse my mind, soul and body of all the excess weight and pain of my marriage. I had a few thousands left that could buy a one-way ticket to the Bahamas. Okay. A two-way ticket. I wouldn't leave my babies. But cocktails were enticing. The drinks would roll around the bar before the first glass were emptied; and the white sands and blue waters would be like laxatives to the brain.

I'd only pack enough clothes for a week and leave the kids with Sharon as long as she promised not to send them to Ms. Ethel, or Alexus and his harlot, for that matter. Arriving in the Bahamas early, I would take comfort that my pole dancing career, would not be on every person's mind that I met.

"You want some?" Momma held the bowl of beans and rice in one hand and a long soup spoon in the other. The smell of oven-baked chicken filled the room. A freshly baked tray of macaroni and cheese sat in the center of the table, and I pushed a small amount of it into Max's mouth. He sat quietly as he usually did when in the midst of a mass feeding session. My eyes wandered across the table to Naomi's half smile, and I saw her nod of support.

"Yes," I said, "thank you, Momma."

Momma plopped some beans onto my empty plate and I used my fork to poke them around. Being one of the first to arrive for the rehearsal dinner, I now regretted it. I figured since I was already here, I might as well just pretend to enjoy it.

Momma got up every two or three minutes and dumped more food on any plates that stayed clean for longer than a minute. She was in a good mood. She smiled three or four times, and that that left me feeling confused about whether or not she was happy about Alex's and my separation. Or was her smirk a genuine tactic for support?

And Ms. Ethel called *me* petty? I was here in the same quarters as my mother and father. I didn't say anything to signal such a thing, and I was not holding any grudges. Sitting in my parents' dining room was proof of that.

Pharah suddenly shot out of her chair and studied the guests at the table.

"We can all fit around the table," Pharah said, "and give the happy couple our well wishes." Taking her seat, she pushed her empty plate to the side and said, "I'll go first."

"That's a great idea," Rachel chimed in after checking her watch.

I stuffed another spoon of rice into Max's mouth and moved my eyes around the room to check for an opportunity to excuse myself.

There wasn't anything nice I had to say about being married, especially in light of my dilemma. Alex hadn't found his way back home. By the time we got around to Momma, it was all she could do not to weep. She looked old now. I remembered her from the days of my wedding when I looked to her for instructions on how to be a good wife. There really wasn't much I could learn since Momma played the roles of both husband and wife.

Momma pitched the same, "That's it, 'til death do you part,'" speech and her eyes landed on me. I shoved another handful of rice in Max's mouth.

"These marriages nowadays," she said, "don't outlast the honeymoons."

Pastor was at the head of the table, and he sounded off with, "Preach, sister," after Momma spoke.

Pharah became giddy as she usually was and pulled out a two-page, handwritten novel.

Turning to Max, whose mouth opened for another rice drop, I cupped my hand over his mouth, and yanked him forward to my chest and asked, "Are you okay, baby?"

Max pushed at my chest to move me away, but I held him still and only left enough space for breathing room. No one at the table could make out the words I heard him say, "Moooo, Mommy."

Looking around the table, I gave the *I'm okay-we're okay, but he's ready to leave* smile. Rachel's eyes widened as if showing sympathy.

"He's not feeling too good, guys," I said. Quick as I could, I lifted Max onto my hips, and said, "It's okay, sweetie," nodding while he tried to read me. I tucked Max's head over my shoulder and slipped out of the dining room before gathering my things and leaving.

CHAPTER 38 Naomi

THERE WAS NO WAY I INTENDED TO EAT even if Momma tried to ram the food through my nostrils. Red beans, macaroni and cheese, deviled eggs, baked and fried chicken typically would have moved the hair strands in my nose on any given day, but not this one. My appetite fizzled even before Bethany snatched her kids to go home like the house was on fire. It didn't stop the progress being made on the night before my wedding. Everyone was excited about the *big day* except me.

Not a sad face amidst the cheerful ones, no one noticed my counterfeit smile. Momma's gospel music played from her radio. I was surrounded by loved ones who didn't see me or what I loved. I assigned them to be as forged as my faux face. Every once in a while, Rachel looked at me almost like she knew something, but wouldn't say. So I calculated in my head how to make my marriage work for at least two or three years. Unless the world came to an end, nothing else could have kept it from moving forward.

Jessa wouldn't hurt as much as I, since she wouldn't know much about her daddy at that age. I didn't know mine until I found out I was pregnant. Meanwhile, we lived under the same roof all my life. Rachel looked at me again, and so did Pharah. I picked my fork into the plate of chicken, and tossed the slab of breast around until their eyes moved away from me.

Momma who was focused on us at the table said, "This is family," with her mouth full again. It made me want to throw up, and then I could tell her that's not how a decent woman eats. Pastor was done with his plate, and wouldn't let the conversation between Raymond and him go. Andre kept going in and out of the kitchen, with his empty plate in hand while continuously mumbling.

Norman was seated across the table, resting his back against the chair like his meal had just defeated him. "I'd like to propose a toast," he said, raising his right hand up in the air, with a proud and powerful voice.

Momma had a lump on the side of her mouth as she dropped the spoon on the plate. "Stand up," Momma said. "Stand, boy."

Norman stood and held his wine glass so high, it clanked into the chandelier, "Sorry," he said meekly.

"Just go ahead," Momma urged.

I wasn't sure which expression I should make since Norman hadn't given me any indication how he was feeling. I presented my teeth just in case, and was prepared for applause and laughter, which certainly came my way.

Norman's broad fingers clutched the glass tightly. "I would like to thank my family, who supported me during the hard work I did in the past few years to better myself," he said. "I'm embarking on the toughest experience of my life with one of the only persons I trust." Norman turned to me. "And we all know it isn't easy," he said with a groan.

I kept my beaming smile in check while he went on with his speech. He was the center of the attention. After he finished, he plopped back down in his seat and played karate with his dinner.

"Naomi?" Momma said, hinting that I should speak. Instead, I rubbed my fingers on my eight-month belly and began to whimper.

"Oh, look," Elsie said. She was seated across the table with crumbs scattered about her face when she jerked her body over the table to moonlight over me. "The baby's kicking so she can't say anything," she explained.

I looked at Pharah who rolled her eyes up toward the ceiling. Placing my hand on my back, I was ready to assume the baby kick position. Elsie got onto her feet and looked about the room, but had her back facing Pharah.

"I'll say something," she said. Sharp and direct, she spoke clearly for the seated guests to hear. "Whether it's for love or not," she said, "we eventually learn to adapt to change." No one uttered a word even after Elsie took her seat. The silence may have killed my jitters temporarily, but it failed to banish my sense of doom when I thought of the wedding. Thanks, Elsie. My life saver.

CHAPTER 39 Pharah

THE CANDIES FOR THE WEDDING FAVORS WERE all but gone, and so was anything nice I had left to say about Elsie. Not that there was anything to say anyway. *Dear Lord forgive me. Again.* She was unapologetic. I had to tiptoe around her conniving, manipulative actions, and she showed no remorse, and had no apologies and I was supposed to pretend right along with her.

"Your kids are adorable," I said as she let me into my parents' home tonight.

Her reply? "Aren't they?"

Determined to prove her friendship wasn't missed, I stuck to my intent and proceeded to make the wedding favors. Raymond suggested a bright idea to have Elsie's kids and nieces help, but they did more snacking than helping. I bought clear, pocket-sized boxes for assorted chocolates and candy mixtures. No more candies to tag onto the miniature bags, I spent more hours finishing the last minute preparation of the wedding than I did thinking about being stood up. I'll never do another dating website again.

What was I even thinking to take such a drastic step? I had trouble with everyday men who casually walked by me. What in the world made me think they'd want to date me before we'd even met?

"Here's some more," said Raymond.

He walked into Momma's living room where I'd been working up my magic. "The box of jelly beans will have to do." I sat on the edge of the sofa and threw my back against the pillow in defeat.

"I've counted at least one hundred and fifty, but we still need about forty more," I said.

A gentle shake from the sofa was the first sign that Raymond had taken refuge next to me. The dishes clanked in the kitchen. I heard Momma speaking on the telephone, saying, "Norman loves my daughter, and he practically begged us to let him marry her."

Pastor was in the next room by the sound of it, and watching the eleven o'clock news. I covered my mouth with my hand to conceal a yawn. Raymond's chin was buried under his arm.

"I have to be at the church by nine-thirty a.m." I said. I gave the instructions to the bridal party and told the choir to be on time or they wouldn't be participants. The deejay, the food, and Naomi were ready to go.

Stretching my arms over my head, I closed my eyes to digress.

Mrs. Adeline, Mary and Audrey had prepared meals from the list I provided. I'd have to make two trips in order to make good on the four p.m. buffet dinner. My dress was hemmed and so were Cynthia's and Rachel's. Everything was set and proceeding per my plans.

A faint tap on my shoulder sent my daydream out like a light. "Lay right here," Raymond said as he pointed to the empty space between us. "Let me rub your back." He placed his warm, heavy hands on my back, and was quick to remove my limp body from its original place. He pressed in the bridge between my shoulder blades and dug his knuckles into the muscles of my back. Gentle, yet effective, he circled his fingers around the nape of my neck. I dropped my head forward and didn't hesitate to close my eyes and become enthralled by Raymond's hidden talent.

"Does that feel good?" he asked.

Relishing his hand movement skating down my back, I mumbled "Um-hum." My chin touched my chest and my eyes were now heavy enough to let me release all the tension.

"How about that?" Raymond asked.

Digging into the bones of my upper back, he was careful to keep rubbing as he made his way up my neck.

"It feels…" My words were slurred, but I didn't care. His hand motions put all my thoughts on ice. "…Real good," I said.

Raymond pushed the center of my back forward, and I felt my body jerk as his fingers slid down the back of my polyester shirt.

"Bet your internet date can't do that."

BET YOUR INTERNET DATE CAN'T DO THAT! I snatched my shoulder away like Raymond was trying to steal it. Raymond's remark insulted me.

"What is that supposed to mean?"

Raymond's eyes widened as if he were shocked by his own statement. He picked up a candy piece and danced around while holding the sides of his ears. He even stuck his tongue out like a two-year-old, waiting for a laugh. I played along with the horseplay and giggled as he did. Then, turning the giggle volume down, I tried to sneak my original question back in. "What is that supposed to mean, Raymond?"

Raymond poked his fingers in the air and directed me to follow him. Pointing to himself, than at me, he used both of his index fingers to draw lines of the letter "M."

After I scratched my head the second time, Raymond again pointed to me, then to himself, and used his hands to draw a heart shape.

I played along with his hand dance, but threw my own hands up and asked, "What are you doing?"

Raymond stood up and took the black and white, striped sweater off. He tucked his black shirt into his pants and took his time while I patiently waited. I could easily smell Raymond's fear by the delay in his directness.

"Hello?" I prodded.

Raymond lifted his head and gently placed his chin on his chest as if cradling himself. He removed his hand from his chest and placed it above mine. He again pointed to me, then to him and the heart shapes? Me and... suddenly my heart darted with emotion. "Me and you!" Raymond finally said.

Feeling vulnerable, I covered my mouth as if Raymond hadn't seen my crooked teeth millions of times before.

"Are you for real?"

Raymond cupped his hand over mine, and I loosened our grip when his clammy hands suggested he was as frightened as I was.

"I didn't know how else to tell you," he said.

The scent of rubbing alcohol funneled through the sleeve of his shirt. "You don't have to say anything, Pharah," he said, "I'm sorry I had you do all that with the website, but I wanted to make sure you weren't seeing anyone already."

Opening my mouth wide, I wanted to ask about all the women he gloated over and the girl he once said he was dating. All of those times, he showed me nothing but the distinct impression of what a *taken* man was like.

"So the truth is," he said, "I would like to take you out on a date."

Pushing my face into his hand, I tried to seal my lips from the instant urge to scream. I wanted to scream the words I'd anticipated screaming for so many years. HE FINALLY APPEARED!

155

CHAPTER 40 Andre

THERE WERE AT LEAST ONE HUNDRED CARS PARKED OUTSIDE Pastor's church and more than fifty guests standing around, who, I presumed, were waiting for my sister. I wasn't going to show my face at the wedding even though I wanted to. I didn't trust myself enough to ensure I wouldn't lose my cool again.

Cynthia had already done enough to make my life miserable and every time she came to mind, I felt like scrambling for another hit. Cynthia's restraining order didn't prevent me from looking. Besides, I was heading in the same route for my regular visit to Scooter's. The rows of luxury vehicles were lined bumper-to-bumper like dominoes. The large hats congregated on the steps of the church with members exchanging words, and all smiles, while children ran up and down the street, waiting for the bride to arrive.

Naomi was a grown woman now. She never disrespected me. I wished I could have supported her now even though she wasn't too happy when I told her, "the knucklehead you're marrying has a little too much control over you."

She didn't exactly agree. I could tell by the way she avoided making eye contact whenever I spoke after that. As long as he made her happy, I supposed, However, she failed to comprehend how well I knew men like her knucklehead. But no one ever listened to me.

I drove slowly down Ellsworth Avenue, being careful not to draw any attention. Even with the sun beaming in my eyes, I didn't let it take away my focus.

"Look at the bridesmaids," Shirley said. "We're going to wear turquoise for our wedding."

Leaning closer to the driver's side of the car, I dropped my foot on the gas and circled around the block without a plan. I wanted to make sure I wasn't missing anything. I was not doing anything but giving Shirley more ideas. After a final circle around the two-way street, Shirley slapped the top of my head like thunder.

"There she is!" she said, panting, and bouncing up and down in the passenger seat.

Rolling my eyes from Shirley to the steps of the church, I didn't see Naomi anywhere in sight. "She? Who?"

Shirley raised her shaky fingers and pointed behind my head. "Over there!"

Double-parked, Cynthia sat in her car, holding her left hand with her middle finger up outside the driver's side window. The only contact between us was her finger. I gripped the wheel of the car until it hurt.

"I can get her now," Shirley said, "just say the word, baby."

Sitting in the middle of the road with our car now idling, neither of us budged from our respective positions.

"Andre?' Shirley patted my hand as if she were in a hurry.

"No," I said. "That's what she wants, but I'm not taking the bait." I slammed my foot on the gas, and drove off, leaving Cynthia and her middle finger behind me.

CHAPTER 41 Andre

BY THE TIME I GOT TO BRODIE'S CORNER STORE, CYNTHIA'S middle finger was still buzzing around in my head. She was trying me again. That piece of paper she hung over my head was the only reason why she wasn't kissing the knuckles of my fist. One solution to the unruly vision was to get another hit of white. Cynthia had taken this way too far. After all I'd done for her throughout the years. I helped her move her things when she went away to school, and showed her everything she knew, even if she wouldn't acknowledge it.

She thought she was better than me. She wasn't. Just because she went to school and got all the rich girl degrees, don't make her any better than me. I should have broken her fingers, and dragged her out of the car before I ripped her apart and took off with Shirley. Apparently, she'll never get it until I show her, so the next time I get my hands on her, I intend to leave a permanent mark so she won't forget.

I punched the side of my car door as I climbed out and left Shirley in it, playing with her phone. I had just enough cash to buy a few days' worth of white. My hands ached and my stomach churned from the absence of white flowing through my veins. Scooter was fixed in his usual spot on the front steps and he stopped briefly to look over at me.

I popped the collar of my shirt and eased my way towards Scooter who was leaning against the wall with a straw in his mouth. Snapping my fingers, I hummed a made-up tune to let Scooter know I meant business. It had been almost eleven hours without a hit. My hands were shaking, and I threw out the words before the shortness of breath took over.

"I got forty dollars," I said. "I told you I would have some of that money." Scooter gave me a sucker smile, like he was challenging my efforts, but I didn't let up. He tucked the four ten-dollar bills into the arm of his coat and shoved me away. "Look just take this, dude," I said, "that's all I have, and I really need some right now."

Scooter didn't react much to my request, but his silent stare indicated he wasn't particularly moved by my pleas. "Look, I can pay you next week," I begged.

Scooter chewed on the end of the straw and tossed it around in his mouth like a windmill. I stood next to him, rolling my eyes and puffing out sighs of my boiling frustration. My hands shook nervously so I clumped my hands into fists to retain control. "Come on," I said, "say something, man."

Scooter didn't. He looked over my shoulder as if I were as clear as a thin sheet of ice. I moved face-to-face and looked for Scooter's weak spot, trying to get him to break. "Come on, you old, stuttering fool," I coaxed.

He kicked his right leg against the brick wall, and waved at the kids coming out of the corner store, while doing his best to ignore me. My bottom lip was doing a dance. I didn't need to help it. I knew if I walked away without any white, I wouldn't be able to get Cynthia's middle finger out of my head. I shook my head back and forth and he didn't budge, almost like he didn't believe I was good to give him a piece of me.

Unleashing a rush of adrenaline that launched me within Scooter's reach, I slammed my hands as hard as I could on his chest. "Give it to me man!" I demanded. "Now where is it?" I held onto the arms of his hoodie tightly so he wouldn't take off. Drawing my face into his, I said, "I will kill you, so just give it to me."

Scooter didn't speak. The red in his eyes reflected my rage so I slammed both of my fists into his face. I wouldn't let up as I jammed my fingers around his neck, but Scooter spun around and shuffled with the back of his pants until I heard the crackling sound and felt the black barrel of a gun being pressed on my face.

CHAPTER 42 Naomi

I FORCED MY EYES OPEN, WHICH WERE AS HEAVY AS MY HEART. As soon as I did, the river of tears gushed through. It was my second nap this afternoon, and Elsie woke me up from each one and mumbled, "Your mom's going to be pissed if you don't get up now, girl."

Norman called three times this morning; and the last was to tell me I got him the wrong colored socks. The usual language of love that translated to: I couldn't do anything right. He said the socks I chose didn't match his tuxedo, so he had to borrow his brother's. I went back to sleep after he hung up on me. I don't believe I actually fell asleep, however, since I heard the constant chatter from outside my bedroom.

"See you at the church," guest number one said.

"I'm driving," replied guest number two.

"The service starts in an hour," announced Momma.

A familiar hum of general excitement. They were so excited I would finally be walking down the aisle to marry the man of *their* dreams. Every time I pressed my eyes closed, I got nearer to my refuge of silence. A quiet place where I could daydream and imagine the only two people that mattered, the two of us who, unfortunately, were in this together. I could almost hear Jessa's baby gags, and my coos and goos of how beautiful she was.

But as I lay there in my fluffy, queen-sized, pillow topped bed, still clad in the pink pajamas Momma gave me as a birthday gift, the reality of my big day wasn't sitting well. I tucked my hand over my eye to catch the tears before they could roll down inside my ear.

The tears hadn't helped me feel any better. Rain was in the forecast and sunshine was supposed to have followed by now, but more rain pelted the window. I clenched my swollen hands that could have probably been deflated if I stuck a pin in them.

The feelings of guilt bubbled into my stomach. I suddenly felt tingling in my fingers and toes. Digging my face into my pillow, I let out a scream that was thankfully muted by the pillow's cotton and feathers. I let out another, but this time only after I poked one ear out from under the shield and listened for any sounds nearby. I buried my head even further into the pillow and let my scream out.

My screams sent chills down my spine. My body had grown numb by the sound of my whimpers and the grueling shame of my tears.

What would they say if I told them I couldn't go through with it?

I let out another yelp in the midst of my thoughts, but felt better once I got another kick from Jessa. I rolled over as Jessa threw another punch as if she were in the middle of her own tantrum. Rubbing my hands over my baby bump, I tried to soothe her back to sleep.

I got on my feet to maneuver into a new position, but the surge of fluid running down my legs replaced the moment of silence with real fear.

"MOMMA!" Taking a seat on the bed, I shot back up to avoid ruining my white bedspread. Jessa was not nearly as well behaved as she usually was. She went from left to right with incessant kicks as sharp as needles.

I could do this. Note taken, but Jessa didn't administer any instructions so I had to find another tactic to help me breathe.

Pies. Apple pies with whipped cream on top would have been a nice dessert.

"MOMMA!"

The minutes multiplied before my bedroom door finally swung open. Momma was dressed in her lavender two-piece ensemble. A white flower was pinned to her left breast. I'd much rather have had red roses. Her hair was pulled back into a 90s bun, making the gray strands more noticeable.

Momma's hand flew over her belly as if the puddle I left on the floor was upsetting her stomach. Jessa delivered another swift kick like dominos falling down, when a command to Momma actually followed: "Don't just stand there," I said, "take me to the hospital! My water broke!"

CHAPTER 43 Bethanny

I TEXTED ALEX THIS MORNING AND OFFERED TO PAY HIM TO travel to the Bahamas with me. I promised to pack my bags and fly out of Philadelphia Airport so we could repair our marriage. I suggested we leave at least an hour after the wedding ended tonight and return in a week to start fresh. All would be forgiven. I had Sharon on speed dial just in case he took me up on my offer even though she was running errands and acting the role of my date to Naomi's wedding.

Ms. Ethel was probably drilling another hole in Alex's ear about how nasty she thought I was. She, at least, should have been kind enough to share that I took his kids to visit their grandparents. I'm certain she wouldn't have minded if he permanently walked away from me. In the corners of those same lips where she called me "petty," I'm confident she'd be eager to remind Alex that I "ain't nothing but a stripper."

I stripped for money in the past, yet, but it wasn't something I'd do today. What was wrong with showing off my own personal work of art?

I tugged at Layonni's tangled, black hair while she pulled her head away from me. "Mommy," she said, "it hurts." I slid her small shoulders between my legs while she sat on the carpeted living room floor.

Her watery brown eyes couldn't prevent me from drawing another part down the center of her head. I glided the Hair Food between the lines of her scalp. "Sometimes it hurts to be beautiful" I said, reiterating what *Momma* said to me when I was her age just before she skipped out.

Momma would always follow it with, "if you move again, child, I'll have to pop you."

I flicked the television station to SpongeBob, Layonni's favorite, to distract her from the inevitable pain required for beauty. I spun the white bally around the parted hair and twisted before adding a white barrette to the tips of her hair. Max was down for a pre-noon nap to keep him from driving me nuts.

It's not like I didn't already feel like a total nut. Alternating between guilt, shame and a sense of total stupidity, I dared to believe

163

in love, and afterwards, to lose at the same game. If Ms. Ethel were right, I'd probably have to wait for another year, or two, or three for Alex to call. But what else could I do? Keep sleeping around until the right man stuck? I couldn't. What about me? And my pain? And my broken heart? He was free to have a life, and be happy with his side hook whore while I was doomed to look into the eyes of his offspring each day and be reminded of his promises, and lies, and failures.

Yes! What about me? Ms. Ethel, with your bright ideas that I should stop being "petty!" Suppose he doesn't call for months? Suppose he doesn't know what he wants? Suppose he doesn't know he wants to be with me? And what about *our* vows? Then, who, Ms. Ethel Know-it-all Edwards, who would he turn to if I just gave up?

The chime of my doorbell sent Layonni running to the front door, her unexpected break from the horrors of becoming beautiful. I checked my phone for the time. Less than two hours before the doors of the church would open.

"Who is it?" I yelled from behind the door.

Sharon was too early. Max was still asleep and I had yet to take a shower. Dragging my tired ass to the door, I swung it open.

The bundle of roses Laurent's fingers were wrapped around blocked the morning sunlight. Wearing a white, button-down shirt and navy blue slacks, Laurent gestured for me to come out.

Shutting the door closed behind me, the icy-cold concrete sent shockwaves to my bare feet.

"You can't come here," I said, "you can't come here unannounced."

"You're not answering my calls, Bethanny."

Taking the flowers from his hand, I sniffed them out of courtesy. Then I pointed the flowers towards the door and struggled to stay on target.

"My kids are in there."

Laurent stood on the tips of his shoes to peer past me.

"Is he?"

"He?"

I stepped back, and tried to give myself a quick synopsis of the pros and cons of being brutally honest.

He'd probably accuse me of being an adulterer, of course, or an angry, bitter woman. Maybe he'd say he "understood," or apologize for reappearing unannounced. Then I'd apologize, of course, and accept his apology before he'd leave. Or he'd leave now, then come back every day until I gave in. All of which, by the way, weren't as harmful when opposed to lying. I took in a deep breath and was careful not to speak so loud since I hadn't had a chance to brush my teeth.

In that moment, I imagined Alexus with the harlot leaving our favorite hotel that devastating night; and it didn't take long for the river of tears to flood my eyes.

"Look," I said, "I've made a mistake." Laurent's eyes were keenly fastened on mine. He crossed his arms, obviously, unimpressed by my theatrics. "I need to focus on my family and my kids." Laurent cocked his head back, and bobbed it a few times as if he were now impatient.

"We shouldn't see each other," I said, "but no hard feelings."

"Okay," he said, "no hard feelings." He shook his head as if in disbelief. "I take it, you're working on you?" he said, "Hey. It's the right thing to do."

I backed up to my door and watched Laurent stagger his way back to his car. *Had I worked on me?* Pondering that thought, I watched Laurent drive away. Then I hurried back in and found Layonni's face smeared with clumps of the Hair Food.

"Lay-lay!" I made a detour to the kitchen and dropped my foot on the pedal of the kitchen garbage can before watching the lovely red roses dive in. I dampened the ends of the dish rag upon returning to the greasy toddler. The doorbell chimed again and stopped me in my tracks.

He was not going to take no for an answer. I shouldn't have gone out that night. I couldn't fix my marriage. He knew where I lived. My nosy neighbors would somehow report that to someone who knew Ms. Ethel, and she'd make sure to report it to her no good son. Wiping the dish rag over the chubby toddler's face, I pretended the doorbell wasn't really ringing. The inevitable thump came from a child's foot tiptoeing down the stairs. AND NOW HE WOKE UP MY CHILD!!!

Throwing the rag across the room, I stormed to the door and hurled my own insults. "I don't want to be with you!"

My yell shriveled into thin air when two uniformed police officers announced their reason for being there. "Are you a relative to Mr. Andre Crieur?"

CHAPTER 44 Pharah

"WHERE DO YOU WANT THESE?" asked Raymond as he held the first set of dinner trays he picked up that were prepared and ready to be served at the wedding.

The scent of his cologne was light as powder, but masculine as a Cuban cigar. Wearing a salt and pepper bow tie, and a black suit jacket, he was on point with the dress code.

"Put it in the church's kitchen," I replied.

I took a beeline to the basement of the church, being careful not to give Raymond too much side eye so it wouldn't appear I was being a big flirt. He was a complete gentleman. Since admitting his feelings about us, he kept quiet as if waiting for me to make the next move. "Thank you, Raymond, for your help," I said. Speeding down each step, I added, "I really do appreciate it."

Catching a peek of him pulling in his arm like he just reeled in a big fish, he stood still with the tray in his hand and looked back my way.

He's interested, all right. So am I.

I didn't hesitate to smirk. I ignored my shameless teeth and grinned down the staircase without a single doubt about Raymond and our future. I knew I looked great. I got in an extra hour of applying makeup to look good for today.

"You're welcome, my dear."

His kind voice illuminated the dark basement. The tables were all set. White tablecloths, with an artificial rose anchored in the middle of each. The half-eaten party favors were individually placed for each seated guest. More flowers, artificial, of course, occupied a place in the front row of the bride and groom's table. Naomi's gift table was as empty as it could be. Taking a final walk-through to the deejay table, I wanted to ensure the only music Naomi selected was also in place. I moved a couple of cassettes onto the floor. No CDs.

OH NO! Did I pick the CD up from Naomi?

Poking my pocket for my phone, I dialed Naomi two times, but she didn't answer. By the third call, Nancy's voice stung my ears when she screamed, "Her water broke! She's having the baby!"

I paced back and forth, deciding the order of questions that would spill over next. The decorations were ready and guests would begin arriving in a few minutes. There was more food on the way. Everything was ready, but the bride.

"Where are you taking her?"

"Jefferson Hospital."

"Are you sure she's having the baby now?"

"She is…"

The silence stilled me. I gazed at the phone that suddenly went mute, smacking the screen a few times for Nancy to finish her sentence.

It wasn't long before the phone rang again and I dove right in without a moment's delay. "Are you sure the baby is coming now?"

The sound of a woman's sobbing stopped me dead in my tracks. I listened to the voice that was having trouble speaking.

"Nancy?" I said, "Is Naomi all right?"

"THEY KILLED ANDRE, Pharah," Bethanny said, "They killed my brother."

CHAPTER 45 Rachel

IT' HAD BEEN SEVEN DAYS SINCE I HAD SEX AND THE DILDO I'D been using wasn't as bad as I thought. It wasn't the same as a real hard-on, like Carson's, but it did the job and was as good as it could get. Carson offered to drive me to the wedding if I agreed to let him fondle me a little after Bruce gave me "the dog ate my homework" excuse about why he wouldn't drive his daughter and me to the wedding.

"Just a little," I whispered to Carson on the phone. I injected some sass and whimpering into my voice to prevent him from resisting.

I figured Ashley wouldn't see much, tucked into the back seat of his car, and I'd just tell her the stranger was a good stranger because she'd get to finally experience the much anticipated ride in an unlicensed Philadelphia taxi.

I'd have a lot to say to Doc next week once I returned for a visit. My daughter's father was a loser. My father was who he was and would never admit that he was the cause of my pain although I could say it to myself now without freaking.

I drew invisible lines on the hips of my sassy dress to lay the girdle print marks out.

"Ashley" I said, "it's almost time to go. Come get your purse, honey." The clicks of my heels hit the bedroom floor as I took Ashley's pink purse off the bed.

Ashley's hair was held back by pink headband around it. Her white dress fanned out like Cinderella's. She slung the purse over her shoulder, and said, "We pretty, Mommy." I stamped a kiss on the middle of her forehead.

"We are! And nobody's cuter than us."

Ashley twirled around and I did the same. Holding my stomach in, I watched myself in the mirror spinning around like the little girl standing by me. I stole a few of her giggles, and wished I could wedge them between the large gaps of my life that continued to haunt me. "We cute," Ashley said as I tossed around the ends of her dress in unison with her twirls.

I held my hand on my hips and moved my back in and out as I poked the bump of my bottom out more. "Too cute," I said, "now strike a pose, baby." Ashley let down the ends of her dress and stood in front of the mirror and giggled. Her innocent laughter tickled me. "Come on, let's pose," I said.

She took back the ends of her dress and waved it as she twirled.

CHAPTER 46 Naomi

SHE WAS EVEN PRETTIER THAN I IMAGINED.

Jessa's pink fingers shriveled into a fist. Wrinkled skin, and her breath smelled of milk. Her soft, rose-colored cheeks, and silky, healthy, black hair and swollen lips were just like mine. I pushed for three hours, but it felt like an eternity. Norman held my hand like he was supposed to, and I took the opportunity after I heard Jessa's very first cries, to reach over the doctor and congratulate Norman with a fist punch.

I let the burden of being the mother of his child and the lackluster job he did as a fiancé sink into my fist. He jumped back far enough to scare himself out of the way. Behind the blank stare, I knew he saw my frustration had finally bubbled over and he wasn't exempt from it.

"I don't want to get married," I said, "not to you. You need to change."

Norman glanced at the doctor who snailed her way out the room, and fear showed in his posture as if it really had nothing to do with me.

"A lot of things are going to have to change," I said, "right, Jessa?"

I was not emptying my back bedroom in Momma's house as she planned because the wedding was off, and there wouldn't be any rescheduling. If she threw Jessa and me out, I would make room for my baby and me at Cynthia's. I saved enough cash to last me a few weeks, and I was ready to go back to work sooner than planned, if need be.

I gave the rose-colored cheeks a soft kiss before reporting back to my discipline. "And her name's Jessa."

Unapologetic for my aggressive actions and behavior, I rocked Jessa forward and back in my arms, being careful not to let her sense the tension. "It's now all about you," I finished, nearly gloating over the doll-sized little heartbreaker.

"It's all about you," I repeated.

CHAPTER 47 Bethanny

MOMMA DIDN'T SCREAM NEARLY AS LOUD AS PASTOR DID ONCE I said, "Andre's dead."

Momma's anticipation to break the news of Naomi's labor after I telephoned her was cut short by my god-awful news. The blood-curdling screams gave me chills. My own tears of mourning were overshadowed by the hurt my parents must have endured.

The police said Andre didn't have a chance when a bullet was lodged in his brain. I spared Momma the grim details, but had to tackle my own struggle to rid my mind of the depiction of what happened in my head. Sitting outside Jefferson Hospital, I hunched over on the cold bench with Max on my lap and Layonni leaning against my numb right arm. I counted forty-two members of Pastor's church who either stopped by to give me a hug while others whispered, "It's going to be okay," or "I'm so sorry for your loss."

I caught a few frightened glares when I unexpectedly replied, "Will it?"

I did wonder. Would it be okay? I had no clear plan as to what to do next, so I prayed quietly that the night would fall and reignite some life back into me. I didn't have it in me to call anyone else, even though everyone in my family had already arrived, and were dressed, naturally, for Naomi's wedding.

What would his daughters do without their father? And his wife? I lowered my head, partially resting it on my own shoulder and let the brewing pressure inside me find release through my tears. A family torn apart... now what?

My salty tears weren't slowing down. My face felt tight against the cool breeze of the night. The blood-curdling screams from Momma sounded again. I shook my head in full support of her grief. I was slightly comforted by our connection in the love we shared to the same man she birthed, and I almost felt like I belonged. Looking toward the skies to shut out the world, the stars were as bright as stage lights pointed on me. Momma's screech was muffled by the sound of prayers.

Closing my own eyes for fear of what I might feel next, since everything around me didn't feel real, I inhaled a few deep breaths before the thump from a car door being shut snapped my eyes open.

Alex was like a stick figure as he approached. His eyes were puffy and he buried his face in the palms of his hands. His shadowy figure overwhelmed my dampened, beaten spirit. I made a fist to stop shaking, and let every pain that ever ached inside me sing a melody through my vocal cords. Alex folded his arm around my neck. His scent, the one I'd been missing, rekindled the anger that once boiled inside me.

"So sorry about your brother," Alex whispered. My hiccup disrupted his flow of words. "I'm here for you," he said, "and I'm so sorry."

Alex held still and I snuggled my head under his chin. I wanted to tell him how difficult it had been without him and how much I'd missed him. And how awful he was to cheat, and lie, and how he represented nothing to me now, but pain. But I didn't. None of it mattered at that moment. None of it changed yesterday, or this very moment where I sat with my three children on a cold bench in front of a hospital after learning of the untimely demise of my brother. The flood of tears streaming down my face did more than relieve some stress; it served as a catharsis, and now cleansed me.

CHAPTER 48 Cynthia

"I'M SORRY, MONIQUE," I SAID.

I forced a hug out of her limp body. She didn't lift any parts of her upper extremities, as I expected from a person whose only job at that moment was to mourn. She nodded here and there, giving me the impression she was all ears, but I knew she wasn't. "If you need anything, please call me," I added as I set my business card on the coffee table beside her.

"I'm going to find out who did this," I added, instantly recognizing how moot my actions were since Monique's eyes suggested she'd much rather have had Andre.

Holding together my pride and dignity after I stepped into Momma's kitchen, I took a seat at the kitchen table and joined more sad faces. The scent of fresh banana pudding seeped from the foiled pan centered on the table. Seeing the smug stare from Andre's mistress kicked my guilt into full gear.

Perhaps I could have run to my empty refuge, but the stillness from inside it led me face-to-face with the person who created the whole mess. Had I judged him too harshly? Was I too hard on the choices he made, for which he may not have been able to control? Should have I done more to help him? Maybe then, he'd have had a better chance.

I was plagued with the need for a second bite of the apple.

Momma stood beside the kitchen sink while Shirley rubbed her back and whispered something in her ear.

Sandwiching my hands together, I rubbed them until the sweat felt dry. I got up from the table, and pushed in the wooden chair, very slowly. I eventually made my way out to my car and let my head thump on the wheel as I screamed out what I was really feeling. *I am sorry!*

But maybe his death was for the best, by ending Momma's pain in her speculation about his future permanently.

CHAPTER 49 Pharah

PEOPLE WERE PRACTICALLY SITTING ON TOP OF ONE ANOTHER in the living room of my parents' home since it was where Momma wanted to have the repass. She buried Andre in a white suit, his *baptismal suit,* as he called it. He often bragged about it and even referred to it as his "pimped-out saint suit."

The man I saw in the open silver casket didn't look anything like Andre. He looked more like a light gray, clay figure mannequin posing as Andre.

I was prepared to say a prayer before everyone left tonight since Momma and Pastor were both seemingly in another place. Momma said, "Give me his car keys," even though Momma didn't drive.

She pretended that the tears running down her face were "from onions, Pharah" or so she claimed. "I'm okay," she tried to reassure me, but I knew she wasn't. Must be hard to lose a child when he wasn't even ill and you're not prepared for it. I tried to tell her that God doesn't make mistakes, and that made me cry because I was scared to think that maybe He really does sometimes, but it's so much easier to say He doesn't.

I took several moments here and there to think about the good times we shared, and made promises to Andre privately about all the challenges I intended to take on in his name's sake. I also promised to help support his wife and his children, and try to make things easier for them.

"You need anything to drink?" I asked.

Monique's eyes were as red as her polished fingernails. She shook her head to signal "No."

I heard the sounds of her grief without her ever speaking. It was like being unable to swallow when your mouth was filled with saliva. Panic automatically sets in without anyone knowing where all the excess spit might land. A platform without a landing means you never know where your fear will end.

"He's going to make a way," I said. Rightfully, *He* was the only way I knew.

Monique rolled her eyes. She wasn't buying it. I didn't even try to push her to believe it either. I just worked my way around the

175

living room while studying each of their faces. Naomi cradled her baby as she ascended the staircase to her bedroom, seemingly unfazed by the effect of Andre's death on her most important event. Ms. Angie, Andre's neighbor, wiped a paper towel over her eyes. Linda, Andre's first crush, flew in from Dallas to attend his funeral services. She sat alone, with her legs folded, and fanned herself every so often. Shirley emerged from the kitchen with both arms wrapped around Momma's waist.

Raymond's back was against the banister as he directed me with his fingers to come over to where he was. Willingly, I wandered over to him and he opened his arms wide for me. Joining my chest with his, the tenderness of his warm body offered me some relief from my own sadness and I rested gratefully against it.

CHAPTER 50 RACHEL

"Are you sleeping better?"

Doctor Choi's question didn't come as a big surprise since my sleep patterns should have been doomed by the holes in my life that never got filled.

"My sleep is pretty good actually," I replied. Doctor Choi skimmed through his notes as if my three-month absence voided all previous conversations.

"Um-hum," Dr. Choi said, "so how is Ashley?"

I wasn't expecting that bombshell question, but I replied, "Ashley's going to start kindergarten next week." Along with the fifty dollars Bruce promised in the letters he wrote from jail a month ago, I worked double-time for two weekends straight in order to pay for her school uniform.

"Let's see; I'm going to be a godmother," I said, "for one of the girls I counsel."

"Um-hum" Doctor Choi replied, "that's good."

Centering my thoughts on remaining calm since my usual jitters hadn't developed yet, I added, "I'm so excited about it."

Doctor Choi referred back to his notes. "Are you dating?"

I was fully prepared for this line of questioning, so much so that I expected Doctor Choi to include it with his prescribed medication.

"No." I asked Carson when he planned to reschedule his fondling sessions since he found an empty apartment after being notified of Andre's death. I supposed my sex toys would have to remain on overdrive until then; no bother, really, to me however.

"How's it going with your father?"

The sound of Pastor's squeal once Andre's casket was closed rang louder than my apartment fire alarm.

"He's human," I said, "and still my father." *And less of a man that he painted himself to be.* "And I haven't had any panic things," I said, "you know, panic attacks in a while either."

"What's a while?"

"Since the last time I saw you, Doc," I said. Proud of my minor accomplishment, I stuck my two thumbs up.

Doctor Choi ditched his ink pen and stuck his stubby thumbs in the air too.

"Way to go, Rachel," he said, "way to go!"

CHAPTER 51 Bethanny

ZIPPED UP THE LAST PACKED PIECE OF LUGGAGE, I hauled it to my front door. Sharon would arrive any minute to take me to the airport and wouldn't be happy if she had to wait. I peeked out of my bedroom window while scooting Max to the side.

"But Mommy! Why can't I go with you?" Max asked. His lips were pressed together like praying hands. "Pease Mommy?" he said. "Can I pease get on the airplane with you?"

"No," I said, "Not this time, but maybe next time, baby."

I walked around the pleading child and lugged the two suitcases down the stairs. Then I took another window check from the living room window. Gathering one pink kid's suitcase and two black ones, I hauled them to the front door.

"He's here," I announced, "your dad's here."

The ensuing foot thumps down the staircase only emphasized Max's defeat.

"PEASE, Mommy!"

Standing at the foot of the stairs, "Get down here, guys," I said. One-by-one, I hung a backpack on each of their backs and planted a solid kiss on all of their faces on their way out. "And behave yourselves," I muttered.

It didn't take long for Alex to push open the door. Dressed in his work uniform, he came over to me and asked, "How you feeling?" after putting his cold lips on my cheek.

"I feel good," I said. That's always been my usual reply, but I said it anyway. I felt good enough to crawl out of bed, and well enough to kiss my kids both day and night without a mental breakdown. We were finally in a good place. A place where I could look Alex in the eye without being reminded of *her*.

It's been a month since we buried Andre and Alex has been by almost every day, checking in on me. We still haven't discussed *us*. We just go about our business as normal while making the children our priority.

"I want you to have fun," he said, "you hear?"

"Good," I said.

"You deserve it."

"Do I?"

"Indeed," he said, "when you get back in town, maybe we can sit down to talk about… you know, what to do long term about the kids."

Keeping a somber tone intact, I replied, "Sounds like a plan."

Alex broke free from the door and wrapped his arms around me. I held him close for a minute too long and patted his back to remind him of our lovely, new, co-parenting relationship.

"Have a safe trip," Alex said, "and do have fun."

Imagining the tan grains of sand slipping between my toes, I exclaimed, "Oh, yes, I surely will."

CHAPTER 52 CYNTHIA

I WOKE UP ON JAME'S COUCH IN HIS BEDROOM. My head was tucked under one of his kids' Pillow Pets. Watching the sun peek through the nylon white curtains, I wrapped my legs around him. The only sound of life came from the television with the news flashing about last night's horror stories.

The news of Andre's death went straight through my head. It was just another harsh reality I'd grown to accept. After spending the past three weeks in my bed, with no work, and refusing all phone calls, I decided the only person I wanted to see was James.

I cringed when I heard his name, thinking about the time he held my hands up to make certain I knew how to use them. And the way he postured whenever he needed my attention. His laugh, his smile, and his voice all flashed in my mind.

Jerking the quilt off, I sat up and James kissed the back of my neck. "Morning."

Everything I ever believed in could sometimes become a blur. "Good morning," I replied. Taking James's hands, I squeezed them to be certain I was awake.

Andre can't shower. He can't eat. He's dead, forever.

Rolling my fingers around James's, I dropped back onto the Pillow Pet. James turned out to be a great help since this all started. He made me get in the tub, eat, and gave me a shoulder to cry on. I had to face the reality and no matter how many awards I received as a top attorney in our firm, it could all go away in a fast blink.

"Stop dwelling on it," James said, "and let your heart heal. You didn't kill your brother, so stop beating yourself up."

Late last night as we lay in bed, I made small progress in our future together. He made dinner: spaghetti and meatballs. After dinner, he lit candles in the bedroom to help ease my mind. He rubbed my big and little toes and tickled them too, saying it was supposed to relax me.

"Our kids will know," he said, "when we have them." He lifted his head and locked his eyes on mine. I rested my face on his chest and listened to his heart beating. "No matter what our flaws are," he said, "it doesn't take us out of the running. We all have flaws." He swiped his hand over my cheek. "You can just accept them, or not," he said.

Playing with his statements was part of a sick payback. I allowed the reality of his words to marinate deep inside my toughest organ: my brain.

Rather than debating the facts, I decided on a more sensible response and challenged myself to shut up instead.

Join our mailing list.

Get updated and new release information.

www.tdgiddensauthor.com

twitter @tdgiddensauthor

More titles by T.D. Giddens

21 Questions I Asked Before I Ran Down To Child Support Court!

*Benching The Court scheduled release (*June 2015):

Micheline (December 2015)

Share your thoughts about this novel.. *write a review!*